My Sister, Esther

My Sister, Esther

by Martha Baillie

Turnstone Press

Turnstone Press gratefully acknowledges the assistance of the Canada Council and the Manitoba Arts Council.

Cover photograph: *Portrait d'une femme seule*
              by Christina MacCormick

Design: Manuela Dias

This book was printed and bound in Canada by Kromar Printing for Turnstone Press.

Canadian Cataloguing in Publication Data

Baillie, Martha, 1960–

ISBN 0-88801-200-4

I. Title.

PS8553.A45M9 1995   C813'.54   C95-920198-X
PR9199.3.B34M9 1995

for Christina and my parents

Table of Contents

Acknowledgements

I would like to thank Jonno for his nearly bottomless patience, Christina for her unshakeable faith and invaluable editing, my parents for their support and affection. I am grateful to everyone at Turnstone Press for their hard work and warmth. I thank the following friends who read passages and commented with care: Neil MacCormick, Mark Abley, Annie Beer, Theo Hersh, Alex McElligott, Batsheva, Bert Simpson, Cynthia Holz, Anne Michaels. I would also like to thank Anne Egger, Ingrid Mohr, Denise Drago, Harriet Eastman and Jennifer Wilton for their encouragement and friendship.

'Can't get that tune
out of my head,'

Can't get that tree
out of

some place in me.
And don't want to:

—Denise Levertov

I

I can't prove any of this is true. My father would prefer I write about other people's lives. But I can't allow what my sister Esther lived through to be forgotten. He will never understand her struggle. He was born in an era of empire and strength, when "character" was acquired by submitting to humiliation or imposing it on others. Daughters belonged to their fathers. Only madmen and artists examined the feelings hidden in their navels—that shrivelled knot of skin that once connected them to their mothers.

We stretched ourselves over my father's beliefs, our lives taut as the surface of a drum. Our fear was cold but felt hot. The way your skin burns, all the blood rushing to save it, when you jump into an autumn lake.

All I can tell you is what I remember and what I imagine occurred when I wasn't there. Let me begin.

In the Deep Grass

Muriel is proud of her bones. She looks at Esther's pink cheeks and soft hands. Esther's bones don't protrude the way Muriel's do. Muriel's hands are just like her father's, and so are her feet. She and her daddy sit on the rocks of Georgian Bay and compare toes. Muriel likes to spread hers apart and check for black goo. At the cottage she doesn't have to wear shoes. She checks between her father's toes. He doesn't have as much and his toes won't spread easily. "Can you do this?" he asks, pressing his toes against the rock, making them fold in on themselves, like worms.

Esther's eyes are blue. She sits on the teeter-totter in her ricrac dress and stares up at the sky. She can't hear Muriel because she's staring at the sky. That's why her eyes are blue.

Esther watches her father laying out stamps on a sheet of newspaper. He has opened the large maroon album. The stamps have teeth. Each tooth is white, like the one that fell out of her mouth and that she hid in an envelope beneath her pillow. The orderly stamps squat in rows. She reaches; when she opens her fingers a red one lies in her palm and she begins to count its teeth.

"Oh," her father says, "so you like that one, do you?" He takes the stamp from her and holds it to the light. "It's a beautiful red, isn't it?" He puts her stamp on the table and takes another. "How about this one? Isn't this one bright?"

The stamp at the end of her father's finger is large, even larger than the one now in her hand again. She has three more sides of teeth to count on her stamp. She likes to count.

"How about this one? You like the bright ones, don't you?" She looks up, her head full of counting. "I thought you liked the bright ones. I thought you'd like this one," he is saying. Her father's eyes have hardened, his mouth closed; his eyebrows crouch.

She looks at the bright red stamp in her hand. She does not know what to say. "Teeth," she says at last.

In the city the dining room is dark, caught in the centre of the house, between the living and the sitting rooms.

"Damn. The candles won't light." Muriel strikes another match. She is twelve years old and Esther fourteen.

"Do you always eat with candles?" asks Muriel's friend from next door. "Do you always eat green salad?"

"Yup. My mother likes candles, and she lived in France and in France they eat salad all the time."

Muriel's mother says that in France they have something called *a sense of aesthetics*. Her mother wishes more people in North America had a sense of aesthetics. "She'd like to perform open heart surgery on North America," says Muriel's father, "and use France as her knife." Instead his wife gets up half an hour early to eat breakfast alone, in the living room, next to the windows that look out on the forsythia. In spring tiny yellow blossoms cover the bush. She has explained it is because of the windows and the bush that she eats in the living room. "Personally," says Muriel's father, "I always thought the French were snobs." Muriel's father speaks French to taxi drivers in Montreal and reads both sides of the cereal box. He knows words neither of his daughters know, though they attend a private French school. The school costs a lot of money. They draw maps of France. Muriel's father asks slowly, "How many provinces are there in Canada?" Neither of his daughters can say. He asks, "What's the capital of New Brunswick? What's the capital of Manitoba?" They can't answer.

Muriel's mother, looking up, says softly, "It is not the children's fault."

"Whose fault is it then?" he asks. "It sure as hell isn't my fault." His wife does not suppose she knows the capitals of all the provinces either. She, Mr. Maclaren points out, is not Canadian. Mrs. Maclaren doubts she knows the capital of every state, and she is American. Mr. Maclaren does not see why this is a fact to be proud of. Mrs. Maclaren's tone is no longer mild. She does not recollect having implied it was a fact of which she felt proud. Mr. Maclaren would like to know why, why he is the only one in this whole family who gives a damn about this country. Muriel Maclaren would like to leave the table. Muriel Maclaren's father would like to know why Esther Maclaren is crying, and is that supposed to be his fault too? Mrs. Maclaren suggests that no one has accused him of anything. Muriel Maclaren wonders why her mother cannot keep her opinions to herself. Her eyes inspect the roses on the silver spoons.

Muriel wonders why her mother is not smiling. "When I married your mother," Mr. Maclaren proclaims, "your Aunt Susan said to me: 'My goodness, David, I didn't know they made women like that any more.' She knew your mother was a lady. These days they call any woman a lady, but your mother is the real item. She also happens to be the most beautiful woman this city has had the honour of harbouring in years. I should have taken her out more often. It really wasn't fair of me to keep such a vision of loveliness all to myself."

Muriel's mother suggests, "The children have already heard this."

Muriel's father doesn't feel it will do them harm to hear it again. "It was her elbows," he says. "One look at her elbows and I was lost." Muriel's mother's mouth has set in a hard line. Muriel does not understand. She wishes her daddy loved her as much as he loves her mother.

The rain hammers Esther's and Muriel's bodies, their arms, their necks, the small of their backs. They are five and seven years old. The rain crushes the juniper; it fills the air with the dank odour of wet lichen. "Come in soon, or you'll catch a chill," their mother urges from the doorway. They continue to dance. The water becomes cold. Then they go to her. They watch the tiny drops escape from their skin, sucked into the heat of the fire. Their father sits at the table eating cookies, his shoulders curved forward.

It is night, and Esther's mother whispers, "I'm going to help your father check that the boat is tied tightly." The room is cold and Esther has pulled her blankets to her chin. The white lozenges of her quilt dip across her knees, holding one another by the hand, as if crossing the street.

She wonders how high the waves are. Outside her window a sudden light flickers in the woods. She imagines the wet needles flattening beneath her parents' feet as they hurry along the path, over the roots and stones.

The door slams in the porch. Her mother has come. She crouches between the two beds and whispers, "I don't want to wake Muriel. Your father is replacing a rope on the boat. It will be all right." Esther's mother's lips kiss her. Water is trickling from her mother's hair. "I'm going to change into some dry clothes."

Her mother walks out, into her own dark bedroom.

Perhaps the boat will free itself and drift far into the bay, or already, too heavy for her father to hold off, it is smashing on the rocks. Esther closes her eyes and waits for the slam of the porch door and the sound of her father's boots coming into the house.

All afternoon Emily has been sorting papers. She is sitting in her room in her little yellow chair, the one that Muriel isn't allowed to sit in because Muriel sits down too hard. The chair is old. Emily has shown Muriel the crack where the mahogany is glued together. She is explaining that the chair is special because it is low.

Muriel Maclaren doesn't care about the chair. She doesn't sit down hard. Sometimes she wishes her mother would sit down hard on her and make her tell the truth, all the thoughts in her head. Then there'd be a pop, like when a balloon is pricked with a pin.

Muriel's mother is apologizing. "If I didn't have such short legs, I wouldn't need a special chair. I've never liked my legs. You will probably be lucky and have long legs like your father." She hopes Muriel understands, and that Muriel isn't angry about the chair.

Muriel does not want to listen. She has opened her Tintin book. Lightning strikes the window and a ball of fire flies across the room. In the nick of time, the Capitaine Haddock rips down the flaming curtains. Milou and Tintin are saved. Together with the professor they examine the wreckage.

When Muriel has gone, Emily puts on lipstick. *Please don't make Muriel angry with me. Don't make her hate me.* She goes downstairs and cooks the dinner. She wishes she had tinned tomatoes so she could make Muriel's favourite spaghetti sauce. She writes herself a grocery list. Upstairs the papers wait, piled on the floor. Other women keep their papers in tidy drawers. She sticks the list on the refrigerator door. Other women do Good Works and don't think about themselves. Other women don't write grocery lists they lose on the way to the store.

Muriel and her daddy rub noses. This is how Eskimos kiss. Muriel's daddy's nose is long and smooth. His eyelashes brush her cheek. This is how butterflies kiss.

When Muriel's daddy bites into an apple, it makes a crunching noise. She tries to make her apple crunch too, but can't. She is following him through the tall grass. He takes long strides. She takes long strides.

Muriel and Esther, eight and ten, curl in the same bed, the one beneath the light, so their mother can read. She is reading them *The Master of Ballantrae.* The master wears a cloak. The rain beats down, soaking his kilt, his socks and his bare knees. He clambers across the rocks. The room spreads out, large and white. "My voice is tired." Emily lowers the book, face down, in her lap. They hear her feet going down the hall, water running in the bathroom. When she returns the master follows a stone path across a hill. With her feet Muriel can touch her mother's thigh.

When Muriel's father comes to say *goodnight* the door opens. He enters and stands at the foot of the bed. "You two girls are lucky to have such a generous mother. Not every woman would read to her children for so long. Your mother's voice must be getting sore."

Muriel's mother informs him, "My voice is not sore."

Muriel wonders whether her mother will continue to read, now that her father has come. She wonders if one day she, Muriel, will be thoughtful towards others, the way her father is.

Muriel's father fought in the Second World War. In Ireland he bought a delicate porcelain called Belleek, which he carried on his lap on the train. When he reached Toronto he gave it to his mother.

Muriel asks her mother what she did during the war. Muriel has turned fourteen. She is studying the war at school.

"I was still in college."

"What did you do after the war?"

"I lived in New York."

"Why? What was it like?"

"I'm not sure."

Muriel would like her to be sure. "You must know. You were there."

"All painters lived in New York then. I guess many of them still do. It was where I thought I should be."

In the country Muriel's father clips protruding branches. He removes fallen wood from the paths. He rips vines from the young maples being strangled. Muriel doesn't like to wait. She tells her mother it is time to move on.

"David?" Emily calls, but the woods remain silent. "David?" He appears from between a pair of cedars. "The children are feeling restless." Emily pauses, unsure of herself. She speaks as though hiding a bruise. She is blaming him, she knows, for the children's restlessness.

His wife's displeasure sticks to his socks. David pulls at it.

He tells her, "There are deer tracks by the stone wall."

She tells him, "I'm feeling a little thirsty. I think I'll head back with the girls."

David is not feeling thirsty. "Perhaps," he says, "the male metabolism operates differently."

To reach home they must climb through the fields. Esther and Muriel don't like the tall grass. Spider webs cling to their clothes and chicory roots trip them.

Esther shouts, "It's o.k. over here."

"Ugh. Disgusting."

"Oh no, did you get one too?"

"Is there still any on my face?"

"No, it's all gone. Mom."

Mom waits. She stands in the heat, fanning herself with a leaf.

Where the first field ends, the field surrounding the house, a creek crosses over from the farm above. Muriel and Esther race sticks to the marsh at the bottom of the hill. Sometimes their sticks get caught in the quiet waters of an eddy. They shout encouragement from the bank.

Muriel's stick is in the lead. "Go, stick, go. You can do it. Come on, stick." The sticks disappear over a waterfall into the white froth. They re-emerge. Esther's has moved ahead. "Boo. Hiss," Muriel shouts. Muriel's stick nudges up to Esther's from behind. Esther crouches, smiling. She watches as her stick inches its way forward. When they reach the marsh, where the creek flattens, becoming bulrushes and wet soil, Esther's has won. Reaching down, into the deep grass, Esther searches for her next stick. She weighs two possible candidates, compares their lengths. "I've got mine," Muriel calls.

Sometimes Muriel and her father go down into the valley alone, and up the Big Hill. They climb the hill—the Big Hill from which you can see in all directions. The heat is relentless. David glances at his daughter. He does not understand why she has followed him so far.

When Muriel scratches her father's back, he says, "Ooh, ah." Then one of his hands comes over his shoulder and he scratches too. She likes the feel of his large dark back but wishes it weren't quite so large, so much work. She also wants him to know how to tickle better. When it's his turn to scratch her, he scratches too hard, or barely at all.

Esther's father tells her to bend over. "Perhaps next time you won't mislay other people's pliers." He is standing on the patio, his face discoloured with rage. Her friends watch from the garden. She is ten years old. No, perhaps they are not her friends. They have become flowers, sickly sweet with scent, mouths hiding among their petals. As his hand stings her skin she stares at the slats in the fence. And suddenly, now, she does remember the pliers.

The children watch from the garden, her humiliation filling their eyes, carving paths through their minds. "Don't pretend you don't know why I'm doing this," he says. She feels a burning heat descend her legs.

David Maclaren is standing in the hall, a pool of water forming around his boots on the carpet. "Damn," he says under his breath and lowers himself onto the bottom stair. During the night his mind raced, rolled on its side, licking itself, itched. He sees Muriel running to him across the dining room, the crotch of her leotards between her knees, curls of her chestnut hair slipping from behind her black hairband. She is shouting "Daddy, Daddy," her voice loud and out of control. She clambers onto his knees. Her small, warm, wet mouth presses against his cheek. She squirms about, trying to settle herself. *I'm not a couch,* he thinks. *Although, there is a certain pleasure to being possessed, by someone warm and small.*

The water is forming a widening pool around his boots. "Damn." Aloud this time. *And I shouldn't blaspheme in front of a young girl. I would like five minutes to sit and recover; does that seem a lot to ask at seven-thirty? It's the people more than the work. So few of them are interested in my opinions. What do they care about trees or the English language? And why should they? Christ, I must bore them to tears. And why should they see the importance?* He lifts Muriel off his knees. "See that mess? I'll have to get a towel and clean it up. Your father should have taken his boots off sooner."

She is standing beside him, watching him. He looks away from her. *Where did she get those dark eyes? It's a good thing she's pretty, because she's not going to be easy. Men will find her obstinate and talkative. The talkativeness she comes by honestly. Probably the obstinacy as well. She's bright. But there are plenty of bright women who never use their brains. Pretty or otherwise. I'm damned if Muriel's or Esther's mind is going to rot. As though I could do anything to prevent it.*

Emily has come to the doorway. She is holding out a cup of tea. *Look at her,* he says to himself, *look at how perfect she is, how quiet and smiling, a goddess of peace. How in hell did a woman of her beauty, with a clear mind and a gentle voice, walk into my arms?*

Dinner Conversations

At the cottage Muriel reaches across the gap to Esther's bed. She is eleven and Esther thirteen. When she finds Esther's hand, she asks, "Can I come over?"

"Sure."

Muriel brings her pillow along. Curled on her side, she can feel Esther's flannelette back and her flannelette bum. Esther moves her hair from the pillow out of Muriel's way. Esther's pillow is hard. Muriel pinches it. "I don't see how you can sleep on such a hard pillow."

"I don't see how you can sleep on such a soft one."

Outside the wind is blowing. They can see stars and the black oak leaves. The wind sounds cold coming through the pines. The oak grabs the wind and shakes it but the wind gets away. Muriel can feel Esther breathing. She says, "Your feet are cold."

"Are they?"

"I guess I'd better go back soon," Muriel says. She knows she will have to eventually.

"I suppose you should. We probably wouldn't sleep well if you stayed. Your little bed will be so cold, though."

"It'll be o.k."

"If it's not, you can come back."

"O.k."

Between her own sheets, Muriel says "Brrr" out loud. Esther's hand comes over the gap. They lie motionless.

Esther whispers, "I'm going to have to let go now. My arm is tired."

"O.k."

"Are you sure you don't mind?"

They let go.

"God. Why can't I ever find anything? I hate hairbrushes. I wish I didn't have any hair. Maybe I should just cut it all off, or pull it out in clumps and sell it."

"Oh no, dear, don't do that. You have such beautiful hair. Mrs. Robertson said to me just the other day, 'That daughter of yours has the most gorgeous head of hair.' "

"She probably meant Esther."

"No she didn't. She said, 'Muriel.' "

"I thought you said she said, 'that daughter of yours.' "

"She did. And then she said, 'Muriel.' "

"Oh."

Muriel sits down. She picks up an onion from the kitchen table. "Do you think she really likes my hair?"

"Yes, dear. I do."

"I still can't find my hairbrush."

Mrs. Maclaren comes from the dining room, holding the pink hairbrush in her hand.

"Where was it?"

"Behind the fruit bowl."

Esther leans over the banister. The wood presses against her stomach. She leans out, dropping her words, as if into a sea. "Can I help?" They land with a plop in the waves. Someone's fallen overboard. She's certain she heard shouting. She must hurry. "What are you looking for? Can I help?"

"I'm so ugly."
Muriel Maclaren enters the kitchen where her mother is cooking.
"This morning Mrs. Robertson said, 'Every time I pass Muriel I think how beautiful she is.'"
"Maybe I should cut my hair."
"Maybe you should."
"You don't even care."
"I'm sorry, dear. All I meant was that maybe you should cut your hair, if you'd like to."
"I don't know if I'd like to."

Outside the window the leaves of the oak rustle. *A Hero of Our Time* lies open on Esther's desk. A Soviet edition bound in cardboard. She wishes it didn't come from the U.S.S.R. but from the Russia of before. She's read twenty pages and made a list of all the words she doesn't know, their meanings beside them. Now she has to use each word in a new sentence to prove she knows its meaning. She's divided the nouns, adjectives and verbs into three columns. So far the nouns outnumber the verbs. She counts them again. Soon she'll know many words, mix them into sentences that form a wall he'll never see over the top of. She'll line the top with sharp words—knife and glass. Then she'll walk away and leave him shouting, from the other side, "Why are you doing this? I demand an explanation. I'm your father." Even if he pulls out a few adjectives and peers through, all he'll see is her shoulder blade, or the hem of her dress for a second.

"I hate my face. I hate having pimples," says Muriel Maclaren. David Maclaren puts down his fork. "Lots of teenagers," he says, "suffer from pimples, not that that will make you feel any better, but they seem to get rid of them by using Snip. Or Snap. It's called something like that." He's seen it advertised on the Bathurst bus. "It looks like a cream of some sort," he says. "All they do is just dob it on the offending area and their troubles vanish. In fact, they usually end up with some fairly attractive male member of the species lurking next to them, about to steal a kiss."

Muriel does not want to use Snip or Snap or whatever. The thought of her father watching a male of the species trying to kiss her disgusts her. Muriel Maclaren wishes her father were dead. She wishes she were dead for wishing him dead.

Her father suggests that if she doesn't want to try Snip or Snap, then perhaps she should try scrubbing her face harder. Muriel Maclaren will try. Her father says perhaps it is too late. Perhaps she should have scrubbed harder when she was little. He really doesn't know. He, Mr. Maclaren, never had this trouble when he was her age, though he certainly had numerous other troubles of various sorts, the exact nature of which he won't go into right now. Kenny Thomas, his best friend, on the other hand, suffered from terrible acne. "The poor fellow had a horrible time shaving," says her father. "I'm sure if Kenny Thomas were around, the two of you would probably understand each other very well. Probably what you need is a parent who had acne, but I'm afraid you're out of luck, because neither I nor your mama, as far as I know, suffered from this particular ailment." He looks towards his wife.

No. No, she didn't. Except perhaps a small one on her chin. Occasionally.

Muriel is sorry she became angry with her father. She knows she is selfish. She will scrub harder.

In her bedroom, seated on her yellow chair, Emily Maclaren is sorting papers. Soon it will be two o'clock. She wonders what she can make for dinner that Esther will eat. She is worried about Esther. When she closes her eyes she can count Esther's ribs. Her worry suspends her. Other times she feels she is ploughing through thick liquid, a clock tied to her leg like a bomb. The clock has stopped ticking. It is drowned in syrup. Soon it will be two-thirty. Bank, drugstore, grocery store. Mrs. Maclaren lies down. Other women don't take naps. Other women don't have fourteen-year-old daughters who won't eat. Other women work for the United Appeal. She stands up. If she hurries she can just make it to the bank before three. She puts on some lipstick. She will make veal scallopini, and scrape the sauce off Esther's serving.

When grace is over and her husband and children have begun to eat, Emily tells them she has had a frustrating day. She tells them that after she took the car to be fixed she stayed home and waited for the plumber. He didn't come. She spent the afternoon attempting to sort papers. "I feel quite certain," she says, "that other women don't waste nearly so much time."

"Most people in offices waste a lot of time," David says. "Especially unionized workers in government offices."

Emily says, "Mmmm . . ."

Muriel Maclaren suggests that if her mother got a job then she wouldn't feel so alone.

Emily says, "I suppose you're right," and sighs.

I'm on the right track, Muriel thinks to herself. *I've got this problem nailed.* "With a job," she suggests, "if you were wasting your time, at least you'd be getting paid to waste it."

"A great many people derive considerable satisfaction from simply going to work and knowing they are making a contribution to the society they live in," comments David.

Muriel Maclaren agrees. "Elizabeth's mother has a job and she loves it, and so does Claire's mother."

"No one. Not any of you. Takes me seriously. Not one of you has even mentioned my painting. . . ."

"I'm sorry Mom," says Muriel.

"God damn. God damn all three of you."

Muriel Maclaren does not understand why her mother can't simply get on with it. If she wants to paint, paint. David hopes to help his wife. "If you feel you would like to paint then no one is trying to prevent your from doing so, no one but yourself." David says also, "Many people in this world are not understood. Take the Newfoundland fishermen for example. While all sorts of people in Toronto go running about thinking of themselves, one of Canada's oldest and most important industries is floundering." Floundering? He apologizes for the pun, but now that he thinks of it, it really is quite good. David rehearses a possible context he might create for introducing it into conversation at the office.

Tick, tick, tick. Esther Maclaren can hear her heart beating. She can hear the potato on her plate say, *Eat me, go ahead, eat me.* Its white, innocent face.

"I would like to know more about the Newfoundland fishermen," announces Muriel Maclaren. She would like her daddy to explain why people aren't helping the fishermen.

"I suppose it's in part because people don't go to church any more."

Muriel Maclaren wants to know, did he go to church at her age?

"Not too often, I suppose. But I did go to Sunday school, which is more than either you or your sister has done. You haven't because your mother does not believe in what she calls *institutionalized religion.*" David puts down his fork. "The church," he tells Muriel, "does not understand your mother. Though it serves an important social function, it does not understand spirituality."

"I am perfectly aware of the church's noble public deeds," Emily interrupts.

David is not done. "Your mother," he explains, "feels uncomfortable in church. She does not believe people who attend church are searching for spirituality in its finer forms, as she is. I fail to see how she has reached this conclusion, given the infrequency of her visits to the House of the Lord." He pauses.

"Neither of my daughters seems particularly inclined to grace the church with her presence either."

Esther Maclaren pokes at a piece of lettuce on her plate. It is bright green and has daubs of oil on it.

"Do you believe in God, Daddy?" Muriel asks.

"No one, when I was your age, would have dared *not* to believe in God. No one would have dreamed of going on social welfare, or of having an illegitimate child for the hell of it, like the one I saw last night on the Bathurst bus. The woman, its mother I presume, wore no ring. The sire of her child, the man who, as we used to say, *knocked her up,* would probably refuse to work even if you gave him a job. What someone should do is give him a swift, hard kick in the arse."

Muriel wonders whether, by going to church, she could help the Newfoundland fishermen. Esther is staring at her plate. The tomato on Esther's plate is a ball of blood.

"Why," she asks, "is it your business anyway, if the woman was married or not?"

"You'll leave the table, if you speak to me like that again."

"Like what?"

"I'll smack your bottom, if you keep this up."

Esther lowers her eyes.

Mr. Maclaren wonders what difference it makes to Esther whether the woman on the bus was married or not. He is staring at the food on his plate, the half piece of pork, the remains of a potato. He imagines Esther on a bus, her belly distended. No ring to hide her shame. Her lost virginity. Harlot. Slut. Her room, he recalls, is a pigsty. "Your room," he says, "is a pigsty. Only a slut would keep such a room."

"You have no right to call me that."

"Call you what?"

"A prostitute."

"I called you no such thing."

"You said only a slut would keep a room like mine."

"A slut, miss, is a slovenly woman. A prostitute fornicates for remuneration."

"David." Emily has raised her voice.

David has taken the *Oxford English Dictionary* from its stand.

"Slut," he reads, "a slovenly woman. Sloven. Personally untidy or dirty, careless and lazy, or unmethodical person."

Muriel watches. Tears are making Esther's cheeks shiny and wet. Muriel watches as Esther hides her face in her soft, pale hands. The legs of Esther's chair scrape the carpet. Muriel thinks, *I will never be like Esther.* In the stairwell, Esther's feet pound. Above the ceiling, above the dining-room light with its dangling bits of glass, a bedroom door slams shut.

"I do not understand," says Emily, "I do not understand why you persist in pushing that poor girl to the edge. Don't you know how sensitive she is?"

Emily Maclaren opens the car door and climbs into the driver's seat. She inserts the key in the ignition, then looks up at the windshield. Leaves have fallen in the shape of a woman's body. The rain has plastered them to the glass. The curve of the woman's lower breast is visible. Her hips lie open. Rain, collecting in rivulets, runs over the leaves and down the glass. Now she sees only the colours, the buttermilk of the leaves, the dark of the garage. Not black, a blue and brown. Still, and with her eyes open, she sees a white canvas and imagines she is lifting her brush but stops. *What if I fail?* she asks herself. She sits for a moment with her hands in her lap. *These funny hands that do laundry, chop vegetables, clean up cat hair, and ever so occasionally hold a paintbrush.*

She eases her foot off the clutch and the car lurches backwards, tires scattering the gravel. Once her father stood beside another garage.

"Where is Emily?"

"Out by the garage."

Her father has helped her carry her paintings. They've leaned them in a row against the garage wall. Her father crouches now on the lawn, reading the light with the meter of his camera. She feels a sudden light-headedness. Perhaps the sun is too bright? Now he adjusts the angle of his camera, on the squat metal tripod. "They're good," he announces. The sun is beating on the top of her head and the back of her neck. *I'll never paint again, I'll never manage it.* Exhaust pours from the tailpipe. She rides past the house. At the corner she stops. Instead of turning in the direction of the supermarket she drives west. The car rolls obediently towards the studio. *What will they say when I haven't bought the groceries? Supper will be late.* Golden leaves lie on the wet road. She circles the block and steers east towards home. *I'll steam broccoli and fry it with ginger, add a red pepper and some carrots for colour.* She imagines the smell of the basmati rice. A leaf sails into the windshield and sticks to the wet glass.

David Maclaren puts down his knife and says how nice a good meal tastes when you've waited and you really deserve it.

Emily Maclaren says, "Mmmm," and smiles.

David Maclaren tells them a story. At the Bathurst Street subway station he watches. He sees all those poor people who can't make it home without stopping for a little sweet. He feels glad he's not controlled by his stomach. Muriel Maclaren stares at her plate. Her father is laughing. He watches, he says, how they peel back the wrapper, and in it goes, pop pop pop. They can't even control themselves enough to make it last. David often thinks he wouldn't mind a little sweet himself. A nice bit of chocolate, a square of Caramilk with all that lovely ooze inside. Or maybe a Crunchy Bar?

Muriel's father looks happy now. He always looks happy when he's talking about chocolate. Crunchy Bar is Muriel's favourite. She tells her father, "I love Crunchy Bars." David is thinking. "Crunchy Bars," he announces, "are not, financially, the best buy. But then most people can't be bothered to stop and think. Either they've never been taught to think or they're just not able to. I don't recall ever having had to teach myself to think. It seemed to come to me quite naturally."

"Why," Muriel asks, "are Crunchy Bars a poor buy?"

"Think, Muriel."

"I can't."

"I was under the impression you enjoyed thinking."

"I do."

"All right then, why is a Crunchy Bar not much of a deal?"

"I don't know."

"I'll give you a hint. Imagine you are holding a Crunchy Bar in one hand and a Caramilk in the other." Muriel is holding two bars of chocolate, one in each hand. "What do you notice?"

The chocolate is becoming soft, Muriel thinks. Yesterday she bought a Crunchy Bar on the way home from school and she made it last. She knows how to make things last. First she took a small bite, then sucked off the chocolate. The sponge toffee melted into a hard lump on her tongue. Her father would be proud of her.

"Well?"

Inside the paper wrapping, Muriel imagines, the chocolate has become a thick liquid.

"I don't understand why you girls find simple problem solving confusing."

Esther Maclaren stares at her plate.

"God knows it's not intelligence either of you is lacking. I suppose that girls must be different. Though there are plenty of logical women about. I can think of no other explanation. I've always enjoyed problem solving."

"Why are you blaming the children for who they are?"

"I'm not blaming anyone. I'm remarking upon what I observe. My daughters display a disinclination to take pleasure in problem solving."

Mrs. Maclaren observes, "Not everyone's a born mathematician."

"The task I'm asking Muriel to perform does not, and I'd like to make this perfectly clear, require mathematical genius. It is a question of curiosity, something, I was led to believe, most children possess in ample quantities. I've always been surprised by my own children's lack of curiosity. Esther's in particular. I have not wanted to say anything, for fear of hurting their feelings."

Muriel's hands are covered in chocolate. She would like to wash them off. Even if she can't wash them off, at least her father doesn't hate her as much as he does Esther.

Esther has turned fourteen. At the dining-room table she announces she has decided to become a vegetarian.

"I've been thinking, myself, that we don't eat low enough on the food chain," Emily encourages.

"I want to be a vegetarian too," clamours Muriel.

David doesn't suppose it will hurt him one way or the other.

"More and more people," Emily states, "are beginning to recognize the stupidity of eating so much meat. I'm very proud of Esther."

Esther cuts the potato on her plate into four and examines the skin.

"I'll miss those nice ham sandwiches at board meetings. Yum, yum," David is saying.

"I thought you liked animals," argues Muriel.

David laughs. "I wear leather shoes, as do you and your sister Esther, and for that matter, my wife."

"The point," Emily explains, "is that if everyone ate lower on the food chain, soya beans for instance, then there'd be far more protein to go around."

David says, "Nice ham sandwiches, yum, yum," and rolls his eyes. Muriel giggles. He rolls his eyes again.

Esther pushes back her chair. The legs scrape against the floor. Esther has run from the room and up the stairs.

"Hasn't anyone taught that girl any manners?"

Mrs. Maclaren feels it is hardly necessary for Mr. Maclaren to roll his eyes, repeating, "little ham sandwiches yum, yum," as though he weren't very bright. "Everything," announces Mr. Maclaren, "is always Daddy's fault."

In the winter, night comes early. They eat at seven rather than eight. Mr. Maclaren tucks his napkin into his shirt and looks about him with pleasure. He says how a long wait makes the food delicious because deserved.

Esther asks, "What difference does it make whether you deserve it or not?"

"Don't be rude to your father."

"I just wondered how it affected the taste."

Esther Maclaren imagines she is about to become a human spittoon.

Muriel Maclaren likes to babysit. As soon as the kids have gone to bed she heads for the kitchen. Crackers, raisins and chocolate chips are often in open packages and easy to take without leaving a mark. Cookies might be counted. A cake or pie can be trimmed, but she must work quickly and there is the danger of breaking the crust or of smudging the icing. The muscles in her neck tense. What if she looks up to see Mr. and Mrs. Burgess whose children she's minding? Mrs. Burgess will be wearing her green silk dress and clutching a shiny black purse. Mr. Burgess's overcoat will hang open, revealing his red silk tie. Gold tears will hang from Mrs. Burgess's ears. Muriel can't look into their eyes. She puts the plate in the refrigerator. Her heart is beating wildly. She wanders into the living room, into the dark hall, the living room again, full of the dark legs of chairs and the wine-coloured sofa. With effort she sits on the sofa and opens her school bag.

Esther holds a radio. It rests in her lap as the family drives into the countryside. When they have arrived at the farm she lies in her room, listening to music while Muriel and her father argue with her mother over whether she is wasting electricity. She is listening to the same music other people listen to. Through the thin antenna, fumes and clatter, and cement, the indifference of an impertinent world slips into her room. *I have let it in.* She rolls onto her back. Her father's feet, passing in the hall, change her bed into a stone slab. She imagines the arching sky, and a knife poised above her navel. But nothing happens and she lies in a void. She rolls onto her side.

Her mother raps on the door. Esther curls into the form of a parchment, the words of her mother's life printed on her skin. When her mother opens the door, she will unroll Esther and read the careful ink. As her mother recognizes the familiar letters, she'll murmur words of comfort.

Muriel is skiing. She has left the others and cut off across a field. Her skis sink beneath the snow, but she must not turn back. The others must not know that she, Muriel, can feel her will fading. "The Canadian legal system is based on precedent." Her father's voice sounds clear, as though he were standing next to her. If she cannot make it across the field, no one else will. It was not weakness that enabled the settling of these fields.

He guides her: "For decades Canadian quarters have been slipping south of the border, where the silver is melted out of them, until now the Canadian quarter has no more true metal value than the American." She sees a woods at the far side of the field. If only she can reach the trees. "This is a land of parsimony and snow," she recites. "Of T.T.C. passes never forged." Behind her Esther raises a ski pole and waves. Muriel has nearly reached the trees.

Esther has chosen the wrong teacup. It is too small to hold all her tea. "I'm sorry, teacup, but I can't use you," she whispers. "You're too small. Poor cup." Her mother stands at the stove, sliding slivers of green pepper along the hot oiled surface of the frying pan. Esther cradles the empty teacup in her hands. She touches the porcelain ribs with her lips. "I'm sorry. Poor teacup." She feels her mother's eyes travelling along her cheeks, her mouth, her nose, her mother's eyes retracing their path like a person lost in the street. Her mother holds the refrigerator door open while Esther takes the carton of milk in one hand and fishes for a piece of cheese with the other. "Tomorrow," Esther whispers as she returns the teacup to its shelf, "I won't put you back. I promise."

The leaves have fallen. Through the naked trees Emily sees the sodden field at the base of the hill. *How my father would have hated this house, exposed on its rise of land. The wind would have frightened him.* She looks down through the ash for a sign of a red rain jacket, for Esther's yellow. *My mother bought a large house, on the crest of a hill. My father sat in his chair, his necktie smooth against his chest, his shoulders stiff with tension. The dictionary open in his lap, he jotted down words for the evening's Scrabble game.* Finally, two raincoats, the red one and the yellow. They approach the stile slowly, moving through the deep grass. *Esther's hands will be cold, Muriel hungry.* Hurriedly Emily fills the kettle and plugs it into the wall. For herself she pours a glass of sherry. *My father refused to drink alcohol. He would ignore the glass my mother brought him. He would allow no substance to loosen his grip.* Through the spindle trees, the red and the yellow girls grow larger as they climb. *That I should be a mother . . .*

It seems to Emily, as it often has before, that she is the child. Her father is standing between the trees, watching her. The long stiff pleats of his pants will fold next to her arm as he crouches. He touches the red striations on her knee, where she has fallen, and she winces. He cleans the wound with warm water. She can hear Muriel and Esther's voices now, as they emerge from the trees, and she is waving through the window, saying through the glass, "I've made hot tea."

Muriel is seventeen. Her sister is saving a piece of ginger root in the kitchen cupboard where the plates are kept. Her sister calls it Wild Boar because of its shape. Each day it grows smaller, shrivelling on its china plate with pink roses. Muriel's sister makes a bed for it out of a paper towel with a pillow to match. Muriel says nothing. She knows her sister's crazy but says nothing. After all, the lower Esther sinks the higher Muriel rises.

Muriel gets lonely sometimes, way up high on the wooden seat of the teeter-totter. She kicks her legs and shouts but no one comes.

Esther's mother asks, "Did you hurt yourself, dear?"
Esther did not. Her mother asks, "How did you get that scar on your arm?" Esther fell. Her mother asks, "How did you fall?" She fell the way most people fall. She tripped. Her mother would like to know how she got a scar on her arm by tripping. Esther asks, "What else would you like to know?" Her mother leaves the room.
Esther is standing next to the radiator. Muriel asks, "How did you get that scar on your arm?"
"I cut myself with a razor."
"Where did you get the razor?" Muriel asks.
"I took one of Dad's."
Under its wooden cover the radiator, warming itself, ticks.
"Why did you do it?"
"I wanted to see if it would hurt."
"Where did you do it?" Though Muriel would like to move, she remains standing beside the sofa. Her legs refuse to budge.
"Astrid's room at university."
"How did Astrid react?" Muriel asks.
"She isn't usually there." With the pencil in her hand, Esther pokes a small hole in the cover of the magazine her mother has left on the radiator.
"How did you get in?"
"The porter lets me in. I go there a lot."
"Doesn't Dad miss his razors?"
"Sometimes I use a piece of glass or the edge of a broken beer bottle."
"Do you like doing it?"
"The blood tastes good."
"How do you know?"
"I lick it."

So much blood. There's not enough room on her arms, and the scars are too visible, so she cuts herself on her thighs. Some of the scars are five inches long and an inch wide. She has measured. Sometimes the blood seeps through the bandages. She is afraid it will show. She walks with a limp. When someone notices, she tells them she has sprained her ankle.

"If you tell anyone, the whole family will fall apart, and I will never speak to you again."

A Kiss Is but a Kiss

Muriel Maclaren wants to know all about her father. They are seated on the sofa in the back room. "Where were you born?"

"On the kitchen table." Her father is reading the paper.

"What did your grandmother look like?"

"She had an abundant behind and we called her Granny Chiselbum."

"Why Chiselbum?"

"Instead of Chelsey—her last name."

Her father, Muriel can tell, would prefer to be reading his paper. "Was she nice?"

"She kept a supply of chocolate-coated marshmallow cookies in a crock in the basement."

Now her father has put the paper down.

"Why did she keep them in the basement?"

"So we wouldn't eat them, I suppose."

"But you found them?"

"Yes. One of us. I don't remember who." The sunlight dapples the carpet.

"Did you eat all of them?"

David can't remember. "A fair number. Not all of them."

Muriel Maclaren is collecting facts. How did her father get the scar on his knee? A piece of shrapnel. There were palm trees flying. The roots alone could knock a man out. Probably kill him. Her father had thought fast. He dived under the heaviest object in sight—a truck. His left leg didn't make it all the way under.

Muriel Maclaren is taking her father apart piece by piece. His hand clutching a marshmallow cookie, his leg with a shard of shrapnel sticking out, his mind scornful of those who didn't think fast and got killed because they didn't dive under something large and heavy. Muriel doesn't want to put the pieces back together. They're her pieces. She found them, and she's keeping them.

With her father, Muriel drives north. Fields fly away from them like an escaping breath. Her father sits with his hands in his lap. Large, bony hands that remind her of her own.

Muriel is standing in the woods, totally still. The trunks of the trees are grey and smooth. The woods cover the crown of the hill. She can see barns and a pattern of fences below. At the far side of the valley, on the horizon other woods small in the distance wait like a frozen caravan. Not a cloud shifts position. They are piled high and grey, filling the sky. A pale, curled leaf catches her eye. It has remained, suspended from a branch, a crinkle potato chip that makes her think of food. She begins to walk. Everywhere young maples, tiny as twigs, are wrestling for space. "They are the young generation," her father said once. "Woods are not static. It doesn't matter if you step on them. Only a few will reach maturity. They'll soon have to compete for the sunlight." She was shocked that her father didn't mind if she stepped on them, when he had gone to such lengths to save a single pine from drowning, an oak from the blades of a neighbour's lawn mower. He laughed. "I was interfering in the struggle when I moved those trees. But my effect will be minimal, even here. Eventually this woods will grow dense and difficult to walk through." She doesn't want it to be hard to walk in. She told him this. "Then you'll have to cut paths," he said, "or find a man who will do it for you. I won't be here to cut your paths, or to see the woods change." She steps over a fallen trunk. Only at the tops of the trees, where their branches touch the sky, is there wind. A silent wind. No sound descends. Then a twig snaps. Something has moved. She hears the call, then sees a bird flying, blackly, between the trees. The only name she can think of is *grackle*.

From the edge of the woods you can see in three directions. Beside the wooded hill are two other hills, both high, both bald. Together, the three are called The Sisters.

"If you were to go digging up there," Muriel's father suggests, looking through the glass door, "you might find the remains of an Indian encampment."

"Really?"

"The ground up there is pretty hard. It's nearly solid clay. I'd be surprised if you got very far."

Muriel says she's good at digging.

"Yes. You are." He is laughing. "You certainly are that." And he wipes the crumbs from his lips with his napkin.

"You don't believe me."

"Certainly I believe you." He is looking at her wistfully now. "More power to you, if you have the energy to try."

She had forgotten he is old. *I am selfish. He will be angry.* She smiles at him. If she asks a question he will forgive her. "How do you know that Indians camped there?"

"It's a feeling I have. A hunch."

Muriel and her mother draw, sitting in the grass. The charcoal branches sprawl disobediently on Muriel's page.

"Oh, you draw so well," Emily sighs.

"No, I don't."

"You do. Far better than I do. Your lines have such energy. I've never had your energy, or your courage."

"They don't look like the tree," Muriel complains.

"Don't they?"

"No."

The wind flips the leaves of the poplar silver. Silver, green, silver, green. Thousands waving from the deck of a ship, Muriel thinks.

"What does a tree look like?" Emily asks.

"A tree. What else would it look like."

"It could look the way you feel when you gaze at a tree."

"I don't like my picture."

Esther stands on the rocks, lifting her black and white dress above her thighs. The cold waves that slap her skin make her laugh. She lets her feet slide forward, her heart beating faster and faster, boom boom, until the lake is holding her, the water's breath moving along her breasts, her shoulders and the small of her back. She glides forward, confident, barely raising her mouth for air. The shore unnecessary.

When she has swum once around the island she pulls herself out of the water. She lies flat and boneless on the warm rocks, her dress dropped beside her, the sun sucking the water from her skin. Her thighs are covered with broad pale scars no one speaks of, that do not exist.

"Did you see those?"

"See what?"

"No, neither did I."

Esther will set the table. She is standing in the dining room, holding knives, forks and spoons. Her father has been reading to his wife. He has read the same paragraph twice, but Emily doesn't appear to have heard, so he has come to the kitchen. Her parents' voices rattle like pebbles being dropped into a gutter.

"Perhaps you should have your ears tested."

"There's nothing the matter with my ears."

"Then maybe you weren't listening."

"I have difficulty concentrating on two things at once. I can't cook and give you my undivided attention."

"Your daughters seem to receive a considerable amount of your attention while you're cooking."

"They don't talk to me from the other room."

"If I'd come and read to you in the kitchen, you'd have told me I was getting in your way."

"You don't know that. . . . If you'll read me the paragraph now, I'm listening."

"I've forgotten now what it was I meant to show you. It was something I thought you'd find interesting."

"I'm sorry."

"I wouldn't have gone to the trouble of reading it if I hadn't thought you'd be interested. That's why I chose that paragraph."

"I'm sorry."

Esther lifts the candles from the sideboard. Her mother is standing at the stove. Her mother is not sorry. Esther strikes the match. *I'm so sorry.* The words are a form of homage, a tax her mother must pay for the privilege of living here. Esther's thoughts burn in a column inside her head. If her mother touches her forehead the flame will singe her mother's fingers.

David Maclaren stops near the edge of the lawn. He stands with the handles of the mower resting in his hands. Esther is beautiful. She is sitting on the stone steps of the terrace, in the shade of the oak tree. She wears a straight cotton dress—lavender with gold buttons down the front. It shows the softness of her bottom. The grey cat—Anna—has walked over. To stroke her, Esther leans into the sunlight.

Your skin is pure as milk, your hair shines like copper. How did I produce you? David gazes at her. He studies her neck. He calls to her. She looks up and he sees the distrust in her eyes.

"Will you come help me, please?"

She comes to him and holds back the branch of the spruce tree while he clips the grass with his shears. "Why don't you enjoy helping me?" His voice sounds gruff. He is about to cry.

A thin scar runs across his knee, where a piece of shrapnel entered during the war. No, that's the wrong story, Esther corrects herself. His axe slipped when he was chopping wood. *I don't really care,* she thinks. She looks into his damp eyes.

"Hold that branch a little higher, will you."

The white house has a large verandah. Emily leans against the railing. She is listening for the sound of her father's feet on the gravel. She runs towards the stiff pleats of his trousers, and he lifts her, swings her through the air, her legs flying like ribbons from a maypole.

"Esther says we don't trust her, that if we trusted her, we'd let her stay there overnight," says Emily.

Muriel watches the sunlight falling through the white and blue curtains onto the pale rug. "At Victor's apartment?"

"Yes. . . . She's barely seventeen."

Muriel Maclaren feels glad she has no part in it. Muriel Maclaren wishes her mother would take her hands out of her lap. Who does she think she is—a monk cradling a begging bowl?

"We do trust her," Emily is explaining. "But men can be very insistent. Or so your father feels."

"Insistent about what?" She will make her mother say it, spit out the word, *sex.*

"About their affections, I suppose. Their desire."

Muriel Maclaren's sister is a liar. *It makes no difference to me who I sleep with,* she says. *Why should it? Men don't care who they sleep with.* That's what she says. But she does care.

Muriel examines her shins. Muriel will have nothing to do with men. That's one problem solved right there. She would like to say to Esther: "Why are you lying to me? Why do you insist on making me hate you? What did I do to you? What you're saying isn't true. You aren't you." The white and blue curtains flutter as a breeze enters the room. The house feels unbearably still. "Your father will be furious, if Esther goes."

Esther will win, thinks Muriel, *as she always wins, with Mom spread out on top of her, taking the blows.*

Victor stands in front of the apartment's flesh-tone door—the colour of the flesh at the back of someone's neck when they haven't taken a bath in over a week.

"I have to go now," Esther manages. "There's a lecture. Later I'll be tested."

Victor leans against the door, laughing. "I hate to see you look so unhappy." His one arm grabs Esther around the waist. Holds her. His second hand tickles her ribs. She laughs. He carries her to the bed. He is removing her running shoes. He circles her ankle with one hand. His fingers trace patterns on the sole of her foot. Gulps of air catch in her throat. "No, stop." Victor digs his thumbnail into her ankle. He slides his hand under her shirt, caresses her breast. There are hairs growing in her armpit. He tugs at them. She feels her stomach heave as though she'll throw up her lunch. His skin smells both of cigarettes and of the bread he spends his nights baking at the Future Bakery. "Ty khudeyesh"—you're too thin—he tells her. Her stomach lurches.

"I like to see you happy. That's better." Victor props himself on his elbow and watches Esther hunt for her socks. She puts on her shoes and walks across the stretch of linoleum floor to the door. *I'll come and visit him again,* she thinks. *Because I'm soft and spineless and a slut.* She closes the door behind her.

"Don't run. There's nothing to be scared of." Victor has opened the door and stands in the frame, laughing. He lights a cigarette and watches her while she waits for the elevator.

35

Esther steps into the crowded street. People are returning from a day at work. Everyone's eyes discern the subtle change in the colour of her skin, where Victor's fingers have squeezed and scratched her. She slips into a coffee shop. The man behind the counter smiles while he fills her cup. A Black man, the tips of his hair grey, his broad smile turning down in the left corner. He resembles Mr. Selby who was the school janitor. He offers her the cup but her hands are shaking. She doesn't want him to see her hands and she begins to cry. She hurries out of the shop.

Mr. Selby gives Esther coffee and covers her lips with his hot, thick mouth, while she sits on his metal desk. She has turned fourteen. "How about her? Do you like her?" He holds up the newspaper for her to see the woman's breasts rolling away from each other, the soft, dark gash between her legs. The woman is smiling. Mr. Selby's lips press against Esther's mouth. The skin on them is smooth. He leans back and lifts his thermos. "Here," he says. "Have a bit more coffee." The good, hot, bitter liquid rests on her tongue. Then she swallows. Mr. Selby is her friend. He kissed her and now she belongs to him. If she didn't belong to him, then he'd only have borrowed her and she'd be a slut.

She has emptied her coffee cup. "Can I have some more?" He doesn't make her say please, and his voice is gentle. She tells him how lonely she feels, while he smokes his cigarette. "I'm not supposed to do this in front of you kids, but you don't mind, do you? Does the smoke bother you? You sit over here, and I'll blow in the other direction." His brooms and mops lean in the corner. He releases the smoke slowly, while she describes her *friends*—three girls no one else speaks with, who never think about anything but books, and how well they're going to do on the next test. They remind her of her father—having to prove how smart they are. She'd like to be friends with Sheila—the girl with the long dark hair and thick eyebrows, does he know who she means? He pours her more coffee. Once she spoke to Sheila while they were waiting for the bus, just the two of them. But

Sheila has never come up to her and said *hi.* Sheila . . . they . . . think I'm . . .

The coffee will keep her eyes from closing during class this afternoon. At night when sleep evades her, she opens the curtains and lets in the light from the street; the leaves of the oak rustle. She wonders what Mr. Selby is doing. He's probably in bed, next to his wife—a short, plump woman, nothing like the women in the pictures he enjoys. He's probably as unhappy as she, Esther, is.

Mr. Selby's tongue pushes its way into her ear. With her other ear, she hears his laboured breathing. He is standing beside her. She waits until he has removed his tongue from her ear. "I'd better go to class," she apologizes. He sits back in his chair. He doesn't make her thank him for the coffee, because he's kind and has no need to prove what a worthless child she is.

"How did you get those scars?" Victor asks. "Did you have a fight with a boyfriend?" He is frying sausages. "Gavno—oh shit," he swears as the ash from his cigarette lands in the pan.

"Yes. I did."

He turns to stare at her, but he has the heat on high and the leaping fat demands his attention. She doesn't want to appear useless, incapable of work, so she's offered to cut the cabbage for the coleslaw.

"Some guy gave you those with a knife?" He's removed the pan from the burner. His pale eyes examine her face. Is he impressed? By her or by the boyfriend with the knife?

"Yes," she says, picking up a curl of raw cabbage and chewing on it. She has started to lie to Victor, with increasing frequency. Every time she's gotten away with it. Dad has not found out she's lying. At first she expected him to materialize at the scene of the crime and reprimand her, perhaps slap her bottom. The more she lies, she's noticed, the smaller she's becoming. When she closes her eyes she sees herself from the back, dressed in a black coat, shrinking as she walks towards some invisible point on the horizon.

A Short Blue Letter

Muriel has turned seventeen and is leaving home. As Esther watches Muriel drag her large brown suitcase up to the Air France check-in counter, she remembers Mom suggested little wheels. Muriel said she didn't want wheels, she had perfectly good muscles. Esther imagines what's in the brown case: a year's worth of clothes, Muriel's black winter coat, cashmere mixed with wool, tied at the waist, swirling out. *It was so soft. Mom found it on sale and Muriel finally agreed to buy it after half an hour, when I said, Take it. You look so beautiful. It will last. She'll have her indispensable rubber boots. Skirts, shirts, sweaters. No jeans. Mom's convinced her they're common. Or has she figured out what Dad thinks of them: sexy, subversive? Paris. What will Paris do to Muriel? What will it do to me? One year of meals with no sister across the table. No one to ask Dad questions, to ward off his anger.*

About to step through the gate, Muriel turns to wave. Esther is standing between her parents. Muriel watches her. Is Esther leaning slightly on Mom? She looks too thin to hold herself up. Her arms are crossed over her flat chest, her cardigan wrapped over itself—an extra layer. *Esther, your flawless skin. You have my mother's skin, Dad is always telling you. Still soft despite all the weight you've lost, he says. Your grandmother's nearly one hundred, and the skin on her cheek and neck feels as soft as a baby's bottom. Your arm is so thin, Esther. How do you manage to lift it?* They're all waving. "Goodbye, Sweetheart. I love you." *That's Dad.* "Goodbye, Sweetie. I love you, too. Write. There's a pre-addressed envelope in your bag." *That's Mom.* "A bientôt. Je t'aime." *Esther.*

Tight rows of seats, about to be lifted miles into the air. Paris. If I make it. Paris; I hoped I'd hate the first time, when I was fifteen and Mom took me. Because everyone loved Paris and it was Mom's. But oh. To go there and never have to leave. To slip into the language, grow gills and swim away. A pair of handsome, waiting fins.

Dear Muriel,

I am reading Balzac and thinking of you. I am re-reading Proust. I imagine the streets where you walk. You meet people and talk with them. I admire you. I could never do that. I am sending you another two poems. I have discovered history. Aren't you proud of me? I know who Bismarck is, and Cavour. Now I can see why you love history. I hardly dare to believe that soon it will be July and I'll be in Paris with you. I take the ticket out of my drawer every morning and look at it. And every night before I go to bed, I'm ashamed to say. It has a shiny white and red envelope. And my name printed inside . . . . . .

Love, Esther

Dear Esther,

I am going to a film on Friday. Saturday I'll work on
my essay. And Saturday evening my friend Nadia is free.
She is someone I met in a class on Hugo. That leaves
only Sunday. The Bois de Boulogne? I will go to the Bois
de Boulogne. Nadia's brother is a prick. He says I speak
French as though my mouth were full of potatoes.
Should I be trying harder? Antonin Artaud objects to
museums and also to print on paper. A clear idea, he
says, is a dead idea. Over. Finished. Paf. I love you,
Antonin. Did you have to be so extreme? Monday I'll go
see a play at the Theatre du Soleil. I must go to bed now.
It is nearly two in the morning. I love you. Please write.
Not that you MUST, but when you can. I miss you. I keep
counting the days until you'll be here.

Je t'embrasse bien fort, Muriel

Dear Muriel,

I've started on Greek and Roman mythology. Edward's had a copy of Bulfinch on sale. What a miracle.
Oh, lucky me. I'm also reading the Bible. I bought myself
a children's illustrated edition. The stories are great.
Don't worry about your essays too much. Enjoy Paris. I
can't believe I'll soon be there with you. I have a favour
to ask. Do you think maybe we could go to Greece? If
that's not somewhere you want to see, we don't have
to. Would you be able to stand the heat? I don't even
know why I want to go there, but I have always wanted
to.

Je t'embrasse trés fort, Esther

Esther grasps the copper hair with her tweezers and pulls it out of her left eyebrow. The remains of her right brow arch elegantly, surrounded by a reef of tiny holes. The house is always cold. She's taken to wearing long underwear beneath her clothes. If she shivers her mother's eyes will fill with worry—like those paperweights that fill with swirling snow when you tip them upside down.

"If you'd put on a little weight, then you wouldn't be so cold, Sweetie." Her mother's voice glides in loops around her ears. She shakes her head. *That's what you'd like, isn't it? For me to be as fat as you. Or do you just not want the neighbours to see what a failure you are as a mother? She can't even feed that girl of hers, they whisper. No, there must be a mistake. You're my friend. That's what you tell me, isn't it? I'm your friend, Sweetie. The kitchen-confessional. I kneel (on your yellow linoleum floor) and confess to the truth about him (as much of it as you or I can bear)—his ego-size, emotional grade level. You bless me. My belief in you will save me. But nothing changes. In the morning there he is again at the table in the window, stoically reading the stock market (for our sake), while he waits for his investment in you to pay him a bowl of Shreddies with banana and milk. Two days pass. Again, the kitchen-confessional. This time you kneel. What an insensitive man, you say, a scientist, linear thinker. How lucky, you say, there are two of us. We'll form a united front no one need know about. I bless you and we make a cup of tea. What good friends we are.*

Esther examines her eyebrow. It is only fat now at one end. It looks like a little piece of one of the furry caterpillars she collected all one summer. They lived their orange and brown lives, striped, climbing up and down glass walls. She loved watching their tiny feet, their progress—eating through a leaf twice their size. The marks their teeth left. Finally she had to put them back outside, her mother afraid they'd escape.

Esther pulls out a few more hairs. *Poor caterpillar, this won't hurt. I have to. You might crawl by and frighten someone.*

Mr. Maclaren knocks on the door and opens it. "I've got something stuck between my teeth."

Esther steps to one side so he can get the floss from the cupboard.

"What are you doing?" he asks.

"I'm plucking my eyebrows."

"What was wrong with them?"

"They were ugly."

"I don't particularly remember how they looked before, but I can't say they do much for me the way you've got them now. Perhaps if you paint on a little colour. Or is it with a pencil? I suppose I should be pleased some things don't change. You can still count on a young woman to spend plenty of time attending to her beauty. We men should be grateful indeed."

Esther pulls out another hair.

"Don't leave those hairs in the sink."

I'll take them with me. And frame them, she thinks.

She closes the door, sits down on the toilet and cries. The temperature in the house has dropped. *Cold house for a cold bitch. I guess I get what I deserve. Poor Mom: All those meals she makes and I can't force myself to eat them. When she looks at my plate, her forehead collapses in pleats of worry.*

No bus. Esther's gaze travels up Bathurst Street to meet only cars racing under low clouds. The wind shoots up her coat and slips through her long underwear. To keep warm she starts to walk. The last grey islands of ice are melting. In a slip of garden between the sidewalk and an apartment wall the delicate green tips of crocuses have poked courageously out of the mud. A first raindrop falls on Esther's cheek.

Last night a man phoned and asked for someone called Andrea. He had the wrong number, Esther told him. She was sorry, she said. As she sat down she dried her damp palms on the arms of the chair. *He probably wasn't Victor. But his accent and voice. Victor might be phoning all his ex-girlfriends out of curiosity, to see who recognized his voice. That would be like him.*

Once he'd shown Esther an album of photos. All of the women were dressed differently. Some sat on sofas, others stood in gardens. One, she remembers, wore a grey trench coat. "These are the women I've fucked," he boasted. The women smiling at her, she felt less alone. Sad green eyes looked up from a round face above a grey trench coat.

"So you'll bring your photo?" he asked. He was grinning. *His smile is unkind,* she thought.

She would have given him the snapshot if she hadn't caught the flu. Her second day in bed, looking through old magazines, she began cutting out pictures of mannequins and pasting them on a sheet of cardboard. They climbed on top of each other, forming a tower. She added Greek statues without arms. Then she cut her own face from the snapshot. Now it peered over a smooth stone shoulder.

"Did you bring the photo?" he asked.

"No," she told him. "I couldn't find one."

He stubbed his cigarette in the ashtray between them, concentrating as though he'd never before put out a cigarette. When he looked up at her he laughed. "Liar," he said.

She didn't answer.

"So, you agree with me?"

"I have to go. I have a class." She put on her coat. He took hold of her wrist.

"What other lies have you told me?"

When she pulled, her wrist came free. She'd walked a block before she looked back to see him come out of the café and cross the street.

I should have given him the photo, Esther thinks. The rain is falling steadily now, and she's opened her umbrella. *I should have let him fuck me some more. Nothing has changed.*

The Ancien Regime and the French Revolution, by Alexis de Toqueville, Esther reads. The book has been sitting, closed, on her desk for over a week; scribbled on a sheet of paper beside it, the following paragraph: "With the approach of the Revolution, the minds of all the French were in a ferment; a host of new ideas was in the air, projects which the central government alone could implement." Esther picks up the sheet of paper. The room is cold. She pulls a blanket from her bed and wraps it around her shoulders. Two citizens wearing red caps are planting a tree of liberty in a hole in a cobbled square. There's a small stain in the corner where she spilled tea on the cover of *The Ancien Regime*. This essay is due in a week. Will the tree survive, surrounded by cobbles? It would have been happier in the field where it came from. Suddenly one summer, when no one is looking, the tree's leaves will shrivel and drop off. It will die of loneliness in the middle of the square. No, she's wrong. The tree will flourish until the next revolution, when they cut it down to use as a barricade.

She feels cold. Esther sits on the corner of her bed, wrapped in a second blanket. *I won't make it to Paris. A few pounds of flesh would keep you warmer, Mom would advise. A little food would give you strength. Bread and green beans, cauliflower and potatoes. Why not? Everything else has found its way inside me—everything you two wanted to put there. Some cauliflower and green beans. All I have to do is open my mouth. And what if they did add a little flesh? You wouldn't have to see my bones any more, nothing sharp, just a smooth, plump, rosy child. A doll. And for the one of you who doesn't get off on being a mother—a doll with a pretty ass.*

The French Revolution waits unfinished on her desk, while Esther curls in the corner of her bed, reading Anna Akhmatova's poems. "My silence can be heard everywhere. It fills the courtroom," says Anna. Anna, ill, attacked as a writer, her son imprisoned, watches the war advance and turns to observe Esther through grey eyes. She holds out her hand. She speaks of lovers whom she hates. They are dark as ravens. Esther's heart is made of glass, and cuts her when she moves. The windows of her soul have been thrust open by the wind; memories hang like wallpaper in tatters. Esther closes her eyes and sleeps. She's woken by a rapping on the door.

"Did I wake you up? I'm so sorry. If I'd known . . . You need your rest."

"It's o.k., Mom."

"I wanted to tell you there's dinner. If you'd like some . . ."
Her mother stands in the frame of the door, respectful, unwilling to enter or do anything that will anger.

"I'll come down."

Her mother's feet retreat softly along the hall and down the stairs. Esther presses her face into the welcoming feathers of her pillow. She closes her eyes and sees a leg of chicken, a small mound of rice, slices of steamed zucchini. She opens her mouth but the plate is too large. She opens wider. Shards of porcelain fall on the table. As she reaches for them, her mother leans towards her. "No. You mustn't. You'll hurt yourself." Her mother takes the shard from her hand, wraps it in a napkin and slips it into her pocket.

The fields of Italy glide past, flat, lined with telephone poles. Muriel unfolds a letter written on a thin blue square of paper. It has been unfolded several times before and the paper shows signs of wear. She holds the letter to the window to catch the evening light. *Why did you do this, Esther? What have you done to my world?*

"Dear Muriel, I won't be coming to Paris. I've tried to kill myself. I'm sorry I've ruined your summer."

Esther, Muriel imagines, lies in a narrow bed in a room that has been bled. Its colours have pooled into a chamber pot set on the white floor. Her father and mother stand next to the bed. Neither speaks. They're uncertain what to do with their hands. Her father pulls up the chair, a furnishing for guests. A table has been set out in the corner of the room, for plants and cut flowers. Her parents' hands hang.

Did Mom and Dad sit in the dining room, asking each other whether or not to bring flowers? Did they wonder what would comfort you or hurt you? Yes. And I think they did bring flowers. This picture of them standing beside your bed is intolerable, Esther.

Small fields of mustard fly past, and the telephone poles, their dark, sagging wires. Muriel pulls out a cigarette and lights it.

I loved you, Esther. Why don't you do it again, Esther? Properly this time. Do you think I enjoy this?

She crosses Italy, then Yugoslavia, and descends into Greece. The train is crowded with passengers. A young Dane passes a bottle of vodka along the hall. "No," she says. Outside the bathroom door someone has been sick, then fallen asleep in their vomit.

In Greece, the heat is dry and the streets are white. Muriel is befriended by a girl from Switzerland. Or is it the other way around? One night on the beach, they feel the earth shift beneath them. An earthquake on the mainland. They eat cucumbers they peel with a Swiss army knife and slice onto bread. The girl asks, "How can you not like yogurt?" From the top of the hill, Muriel can see the entire village. Once, the girl asks, "Why didn't you go back?"

"They told me not to," Muriel explains. "It would have made my sister feel guilty."

In Greece the paths crumble. Dust coats their toes, and when they look up, the light is so bright they have to squint. In the evening the hills become blue. The air fills with the scent of pines. In the village they dance and drink Retsina.

They're told of the shell of a house where they can sleep. "I'm not sure we're safe here," the girl complains, but Muriel has rolled out her sleeping bag and won't pay for a room. The moonlight illuminates the earth floor and the walls of stone.

In the morning they clamber down to the sea. At night the olive trees cast clear grey shadows on the ground. "They are the clothes that lovers have dropped," Muriel tells the girl. "The olive trees are naked." She'd like to remove her clothes and wait for someone to come, to touch her skin.

A sky of steel hangs over Paris. Muriel spreads apricot jam on her toast. In her bedroom stands her brown bulging suitcase. It has grown larger since her arrival a year ago. She looks at the jam. *Damn the jam. Jam the dam. Deedum, deedum. Daddy eats prunes and sings funny tunes. Deedum, deedum.*

My girl's a corker,
she's a New Yorker.
I buy her everything
to keep her in style.
She's got a pair of legs
just like two whisky kegs.
Say, boy, that's where my money goes.

Daughter be dumb. Daughter be done. Deedum, deedum.
Daughter be fine and swallow your brine. Daddy is happy and
fat women crappy. Deedum, deedum.

My girl's a corker,
she's a New Yorker.
I buy her everything
to keep her in style.
She's got a pair of hips
just like two cargo ships.
Say, boy, that's where my money goes.

She scrapes off the jam. She is losing weight. She left for
Greece thin and has returned skinny. Soon there will be no fat
for her to pinch on her waist or belly. The jam drops, brilliant and
round, onto her plate. It rests there, an apricot amongst green
leaves, caught in its tight skin. She's never seen a ripe apricot on
a tree. One day she will. And blue sky through the tree's green
leaves. She licks the tip of her finger, presses it gently onto the
crumbs that have fallen beside her coffee cup, then sticks it in her
mouth. The crumbs sit on her tongue. She pulls out her finger and
hunts for more.

A small blue flame ignites in the water heater as she turns
on the tap. When she has washed her plate and cup, her knife
and spoon, she rests them in the drainer. The door to the
apartment is tall and lined with metal. It clangs shut behind her.
She waits for the elevator which will take her down into the
street. Into Paris. It comes with a soft whirr, then a click.

She must leave Paris. Stairs climb from the river to the rue de Passy. Men and women are hurrying down the stairs towards her, under white clouds. She has reached the entrance to the metro by lifting her brown suitcase from step to step. Stairs continue to the street above. Along the street people are walking briskly past the man selling flowers and the parked cars. Windows stretch from ceiling to floor; the tall grey buildings press against the sidewalk. The sky is still and blue. Plump white clouds float above the leaves of a chestnut tree, above the roofs of the tall grey buildings—the pharmacy, the bank.

She fishes for her yellow metro ticket. *Why am I doing this? Couldn't I teach English or get some other sort of job and stay? One last year of university can wait. I could leave and live in Italy. They must want to learn English in Italy.*

"We'll go to the cottage as you've asked us to," Mom wrote. "We'll meet your bus in Parry Sound."

Through the window Muriel sees Emily and David, Esther standing between them, then the door opens. Muriel steps out of the cool bus into warm dampness. Esther has cropped her hair. She was released from hospital a month ago and has been living outside Toronto on a farm belonging to Emily's friend. The sun has given her face the colour of a peach but none of its fullness. The skin strains in two pleats at the corners of her mouth, as she smiles.

The humid air presses against Muriel's arms and legs. It sticks her shirt to her father's. She holds him. It glues their cheeks together.

Hold Esther. So small. Her bones hollow as those of a bird. Mom, borderless, asking for softness. *No, Mom. Don't ask me for that.* Every feather on Esther's wings is attached by a delicate shaft. *Esther, are you pouring your last strength into your feathers? Can I touch them? There's a tiny hole in the side of your beak. Hold me.*

A bus, coughing exhaust, pulls itself along the road. The humidity collects between Muriel's shoulder blades. In the small of her back.

They've aged. You've done this to them, Esther. Eating only chopped liver as though you were crazy. But you aren't. What sort of stunt are you trying to pull? Oh, I'll bet it's easy not having to talk to them. Living with friends. Don't tell me they're not friends. You all share the same bathroom, kitchen, living room. That English guy. He makes incredible apple pie. Something else you'll deign to eat besides chopped liver. What about Mom's food? You're finally going to finish your B.A. Take fifty. I'm sorry. That was mean.

Muriel follows Esther into the kitchen. Through the window a small backyard.

"Tell me about this English guy."

"He's a jeweller and he collects old things."

"What sort of things?"

"Dressers. Chairs. He has three fur coats and a totem pole fifteen feet long they brought in through the side door. Two refrigerators."

"Where does he keep it all?"

"In the basement."

"What about the damp?"

"He got the landlord to put in a dehumidifier."

"How?"

"He can get people to do all sorts of things."

"Does he have a girlfriend?"

"Yeah. But she's going back to England with her daughter, in a week."

"Will he go with her?"

"I doubt it. What would he do with all his junk?"

Sunlight covers Esther's arm. It covers half the kitchen table. Mason jars are a delicate green. They stand on the window sill, the light caught in them, the dust caught in their light. The kettle whistles, rips the pattern of bright and dark pools on the chair's back. The white paint is blistered. Muriel jerks her head towards the insistent kettle on the stove. "The kettle's boiling."

Esther takes a teapot from behind a bowl of fruit. Someone has dropped a handful of elastic bands on top of the apples.

"What does the little thin guy do?" asks Muriel.

"Mario?"

"I guess."

"He works at the airport, fixing the engines on the planes."

All right. You don't have to speak to Mom and Dad, I'll speak to them for you. What do you want me to say? I'll tell them whatever you want. Shall I say you're fine; that you're going to university? I'll thank Mom for getting your watch fixed.

This is what Esther sees in the morning. Outside the phone booth, cars passing. Metal coffins chasing each other. Bright yellow leaves, paper thin, falling through the damp air. Seventy feet below, under the bridge, more hunched heads and shoulders under metal roofs, racing. Headed home?

This is the phone call Esther makes in the afternoon.

"Muriel?"

"Oh, hi."

"I'm going back into the hospital."

"Why?"

"I stopped on the Danforth Bridge this morning. I knew I wouldn't make it across. I phoned Dr. Pearl and he says I can come back."

Across the bridge the road would have curved. The light would have been red, green or yellow, suddenly, in front of her. She is holding the smooth plastic receiver in her hand. "Esther?" Muriel's voice asks.

"Yes."

"Are you sure you want to go back?"

"Yes."

And I have pulled a black curtain over all of you. A crow's dark wing touched my shoulder. He looked at me and said, Your blue eyes are pools where people drown. Your heart is a jagged rock.

"When shall I come and visit?"
"I don't know. I have to go now."
And I have pulled a curtain over all of you.

Damn you. Muriel pulls at the corner of her fingernail with her teeth. *Buying groceries and going to class was too much for you, Esther? Couldn't you have tried harder? You could have done it, you fool.* The nail tears in a clean line.

Don't you know how smart you are?

I'm not a yo-yo, Esther. I won't let you play with me like this.

"Esther?"
"Hi."
"Can I come in?"
Esther is wearing someone's blue and white striped pyjamas. The weather in her eyes? Cloudy. The weatherman? Little pills in a paper cup.
Orange curtains cover the window. Two books and a journal sit on the night table. A woman dressed in a nurse's uniform is filling the doorway. Her name is Annie. She vanishes. The doorway frames a section of the corridor. Frames a woman whose breasts sag under a pink dressing gown. Frames a man whose black hair is thin and Adam's apple large. It frames the corridor.
"Esther?"
"Yeah."
"I love you."
"So do Mom and Dad. So does everybody."

Esther's hands shake. Energy ripples from her nerves along the muscles under her skin. They are telling her something she doesn't want to know. The knowledge of it trots up her legs, over her shoulders, down her arms into her hands, shaking her.

From an Asian Train

Muriel has turned twenty-one. She's met a man, and she's in love.

"He's a Canadian, Dad. And a scientist. There weren't any nice artists, Mom. Sorry."

She bites her apple, then pulls herself onto the kitchen counter. "His hair is the same horrible red as mine. And he may put on weight when he's older. I can tell from the softness of the skin under his chin. But for the moment he's lean." Schools of sunlight swim on the yellow linoleum floor. Muriel's large feet hang from her ankles.

"It doesn't matter if he's not an artist," Emily says. She looks into her daughter's determined face. She tries to picture the young man's chin. The delicacy of a petal.

"We're going to travel, in China. In a month, we leave. Can you believe it? I must be mad."

Crumbs lie on the counter beside Muriel's hip. Emily would like to warn her not to sit on them but an interruption would probably anger Muriel.

"You don't have to worry about money, Dad. I'll spend as little as possible. I've still got some of what you gave me the Christmas I was in Paris, and more of my own, from waitressing and teaching French. I've been socking it away."

Hot, in the refrigerator's back, the electric motor hums.

David is proud of his daughter and says so. She has monetary self-discipline.

"I would like to know what you ate in Paris, for so little money," Emily asks.

"I ate plenty."

"I suspect you tried to live off omelettes and salad."

"I ate bread also."

The clock ticks regularly, plugged into the wall above the sink. The refrigerator hums, plugged into the same wall. David takes a kleenex from his pocket and blows his nose. "What's the young fellow's name?"

"Terry. Not very elegant, I know. Maybe he'll let me change it."

"Does he have a last name?"

"McIntosh."

I've allowed a man to hold me naked in his arms. Oh God, what have I done? I want him.

Watermelons flood the streets of Shanghai. Each day more arrive.

"Crop distribution problems," says Terry. Another boat passes under the bridge, its cargo of melons dark green, round and hard. They're pouring in from the countryside, overwhelming this city of which Muriel knows nothing. The Peace Hotel. A park where men and women do t'ai chi amongst plants, on the other side of a wire fence.

The axe is never far away in this city. They fear a change in visa regulations, that they'll be caught using incorrect railway tickets. Only a fool would pay for a foreigner's ticket when regular ones can be had with a little arranging. Days accumulate without purpose. One morning from a shop window a plaster bust of Elvis Presley looks out at Muriel. The warm air of the street fills her lungs, and the idea of purpose explodes above her, a helium balloon punctured by a passing bird.

At night the streets stink of rotting fruit. In the morning more watermelons arrive. They are dark green. They are round and hard. The countryside is rolling into the city. It will carry her out. Soon she'll walk along a road flanked by fields.

The cafés are called cafés for lack of a better word, and because cups of black liquid are served. The soothing blades of the ceiling fans turn. Muriel hates the teenagers in booths, huddled around ice-cream floats, their cohesion.

"Did you enjoy being a teenager?"

Terry sips his coffee. "I did a lot of drugs."

But it isn't ice cream. It's bingjiling and she's no longer alone. In China, she's the West. She is crying.

"We can go to Shaoxing next," Terry says. "Shaoxing is in the country."

When she looks up he is staring at her. His eyes are blue. The blue of a gas flame igniting.

"I wish I could help you," he says.

She wants to run her hands along the wooden trim of the booths, to reach up and touch the turning wooden blades overhead. At the table next to theirs a girl lifts a piece of sponge cake into her mouth with chopsticks.

May 19th, 1982

Dear Esther,

This city is grey. In the alleys laundry hangs crucified on bamboo poles. Pink neon signs advertise coffee. Would you like it here? Certainly not the incessant staring. Do you still go home on weekends, or have they released you altogether? I'll write again soon. T says hello.

Love, Muriel

May 20th, 1982

Dear Mom and Dad,

Imagine mouths chewing dumpling. In every direction, mouths eating. The scraping sound of throats clearing, of thick spitting. Perhaps I shouldn't ask you to imagine such a scene? Picture instead leaves floating on the still surface of water in a teacup. The empty shells of sunflower seeds dropped by the leg of a chair. Do you still read to Esther, Mom, at night when she's home? I don't know how you bear it. Postcards are unpardonably small.

Love, Muriel

At night Muriel lies awake in the dormitory watching the travellers breathe. The West, in beds surrounding her own. The rise and fall of their chests. She is no longer alone but a member of the West. *What is it that I want from T?* They make love in the bathroom, her buttocks resting in the white china sink, and still it isn't enough. The night is warm. A breeze enters through the oval window at the far side of the room. Outside, the river, the bridge, the Peace Hotel, the People's Park wait. These are reasons to have come.

Diary:
B is for Balzac whom I studied at school and for the bathtub with feet standing next to me in this hotel bathroom. B is the black and white tiles on the floor. I've been running for as long as I can remember. I must rest. C is for the circular staircase that leads down from the dormitory. An alphabet offers order, doesn't it?

Muriel squeezes her diary into her knapsack, then descends the circular staircase, to have breakfast with Terry. In the mirrored ballroom they eat toast with jam from white plates on a white tablecloth. She is guilty, guilty of self-indulgence in this land so admirably sober, almost Scottish, its knuckle-white self-esteem ready to spring shut at any second. A sheep, a Westerner amongst others of her kind, she chews her toast. The marmalade tastes good but only from relief—no god has struck her down for her indulgence.

Diary:
We've arrived in Wuhan. D is for Dumas, whom I haven't read, Y for Yevtuchenko who isn't French, and whom I didn't study at school. B is for blank, the name of a Russian director whose name I've forgotten but whose images returned to me in a side-street two days ago. A woman was hanging laundry from the window of a mansion once private, on whose cracked front step a child bounced a red rubber ball; and the yard was growing weeds.

In Wuhan, Muriel lies in a fever on a rope cot, creating the world beyond her door. Flowered thermoses stand in a row on the ground, waiting to be filled with hot water. The roof, flat, with an office tacked on its furthermost corner. A thin man sits at a typewriter in the office. She's seen him fill the thermoses with hot water—another duty. In front of her door the flat roof stretches seven feet, then stops. There's a view of chimney stacks.

Diary:
I'm reading *The Sound and the Fury.* B is for Benjamin, "our last born," whose significance we can't find without a Bible. M is Malraux whose opening paragraph of *La condition humaine* I read at least five times at university and tried to translate. But there must have been something I didn't understand because I only got a B. I hated university when I didn't get A's. So few feet pass. I try to imagine the thermoses outside. Exactly how they look.
I've never read the Bible. Another reason I must go

back to the beginning, to the alphabet. C is for the closest thing Terry has found to crackers. When I was small and ill my mother fed me crackers. K for a kiss on the forehead. B is for breathing, H his hand on my arm.

Muriel sits on a chair on the roof, and at last breathes unlocked air. A glass of beer in Terry's hand moves towards her and she wonders how she failed to notice that her parents, back home, were aging. She is crying. The sunset is a taut red band about to snap. She's a prisoner of this roof, captured by consent. "I must go back," she tells him.

But she doesn't go back. Muriel remains in China with this man she now calls "T," Terry being common. He's still young, twenty-three, a year older than her. She remains with him. He has the fresh skin of a child. She wants to give him all of her. "I'll keep only the crumbs, a piece of crust." But he refuses her offer. She's too large? Too weighty? No. Too delicate a gift? Too much in need of repair? He looks down at his bowl of rice. "No," he says, "I don't want to make love to you. I've lost my desire." They travel from Wuhan to Chongqing, to Kunming, to the Stone Forest.

One morning he says to her, "You're similar to your sister Esther. You're not as different from her, Muriel, as you think." They're on a boat that is carrying them from Wuhan to Chongqing. The boat is very large and people have strung their laundry on makeshift clotheslines across the deck.

"If I resemble her, then perhaps she'll survive. I'll survive also, and there'll be the two of us again." The waters of the river are brown. Full of soil from the lands upstream. They pass a dilapidated wooden skiff, a local boat, drifting in the opposite direction. The boat is used for fishing, or perhaps for carrying goods from one village to the next. Its dirty sail hangs out over the water. There's almost no wind but the current is carrying the boat. A small figure sits at the tiller in the stern. That night Muriel dreams of Esther. But a dream is not what she wants. A letter would say, "I'm well," or "I'm sinking." A letter is waiting in Hong Kong. It will wait a month or three. The following night her dream is set in China.

This is what she dreams.

A truck passes her on the road. Then a convoy of three. A young man cycles by. Two more men pass on foot, and a woman. The sky has paled along its rim. Soon will come the final blush of the sun. *Are you worrying, T?* she wonders, and hurries along the road. He is waiting for her in their room. There are crickets singing, and the air is warm. Stars creep into the sky. T says he feels better and they walk beside the river. Behind a clump of bamboo he takes her in his arms and makes love to her. She lies on the ground, stiff, frightened. *Now that I'm a woman again he'll hate me. He doesn't want to be doing this to me, but he must. He can't stop himself.* His face, as he descends, crumbles. He is going to cry. *My God, what have I done to him? Why is he whispering that he loves me? Now that I'm a woman and have betrayed him.* Her body aches for release, but her muscles hold on. There is grass in their hair and the river flows beside them.

Outside their cabin door stands a single wooden chair. When it's free, T sits on it and reads. He's studying Mandarin from a phrase book. He wishes he had a better book, or a teacher. Their second day on the boat his wish is answered. Mi Ling is nine years old and slender, her shiny black hair cut off at her shoulders. She comes each day and stands beside him, making him repeat his words. She shows him how to make them rise and fall the way she wants them to.

"I wish I had your discipline." Muriel knows if she competes she'll lose. Her mind is preoccupied. How she admires him.

They stand on the deck, the moon immense above the gorges. Far below, the water slips past. "I want to go home," she announces.

"When?" he asks.

"Now."

"By helicopter?" He rests his elbows on the white metal railing and smiles.

"Yes. In a helicopter with huge blades," she says.

"And pontoons?"

"Yes. So it can land on the river." A ring has formed around the disk that is the moon. "Isn't it beautiful?"

"Yes," he agrees.

"Do you think so?"

He tells her that the circle is formed by light refracting in the ice particles of clouds. He explains that the moon travels along an elliptical path, at over two thousand miles an hour. She wonders, *How is it I'm so stupid, so self-absorbed, without curiosity? But perhaps I'm not stupid. I feel I am, because of him. I see a beauty he can't imagine, of an intensity he can't feel. When will I find the courage to leave him?* He turns to look at her. He has a beautiful mouth. If she could make him love her, all the pain in her life would depart. It would walk out the door, wearing shoes. But he doesn't kiss her. He's looking at the moon, thinking about gases and distances in space.

By morning the river widens and the banks soften. A small figure rides along the shore on a bicycle, following a dirt track. All down the deck, clean shirts and pants flap in the wind.

Dear Esther,

What will come of my drifting on this river? We're travelling by boat up the Yangtze. If I had it in me to achieve anything, I'd be at home studying or working. This afternoon T pulled a wire from behind the speaker nailed above our cabin door. A Chinese opera ended abruptly. Are you living at home now with Mom and Dad, or do you still get only weekend passes? I miss you.

Love, Muriel

A letter is waiting in Hong Kong. It is written on thin blue paper. Perhaps it says: "I'm well. I'm reading Greek mythology. I've bought a copy of *Bulfinch*."

A metal gate beside their cabin door separates first-class from second-class passengers. Through the gate, Muriel watches a first-class traveller lower himself carefully onto his chair. He is stout, his forehead blotchy, his remaining grey hairs cut short. He hooks his glasses behind his ears, then opens a folder of papers on his knees.

"I resemble my father," Muriel announces. "I'm as self-centred as he is."

"In what way are you self-centred?" T turns to look at her, his back resting against the deck's white railing.

"I didn't give a damn about Esther."

"When?"

The old man turns his head towards their voices. "Why," he asks T, in Chinese, "don't you travel first class?"

"We can't afford to."

The two of them speak of Canada and of China, of T's studies and the older man's research. Through the metal gate, the older man grasps T's hand. "I wish you a safe journey." Then he opens the folder of papers on his knees. In two days' time he will give a lecture, at the University of Shanghai, on the movement of molecules. Along the deck, men and women are taking down their laundry, folding it in piles.

Muriel whispers, "Kiss me."

"Not here."

"Where, then?"

"I don't know."

She chips a flake of white paint off the railing and watches it fall. Far below, the brown water curls and glides along the side of the boat. She imagines Esther swimming in Georgian Bay, her pale arms, that seem to have no muscle, pulling her smoothly through the cold water. "When will you kiss me?"

"Soon."

"Where will we go when we leave this boat? I'm so tired of being stared at."

Dear Mom and Dad,

Yesterday they led me into first class, so I could take
a shower. In second class the women bathe together,
using buckets. I wasn't sorry to escape. They find me
odd enough with my clothes on. I wish you could send
news. How's Esther? Does she go out on her own? How
hard it must be to feel everything reverberate inside
oneself so strongly. Poor Esther. I'll write soon. Hope
you're both well.

Love, Muriel

They leave the boat in the city of Chongqing. The city is clamped
to the face of the mountain, overlooking the river. Coal dust has
seeped into the pores of the tall buildings that crowd along the
streets. Though they're dirty Muriel loves the buildings, because
they've resisted. The government has failed to build boulevards
from these winding streets on the mountain face.

They sit at a stall, eating eggplant. The day's accumulated
heat presses against their skin. The air is still. Muriel asks T,
"How many of the American presidents can you name?" His
sweating forehead glistens. He names seven, and she asks him
to explain the founding of Israel, how the war began in Vietnam,
and who was Pol Pot. He knows all of this, and patiently explains.
She knows nothing of politics past the year 1918. The eggplant
burns their mouths. The street smells of acrid coal fires. Ribbons
of people unfurl along the sidewalks.

A stranger, an Oriental schoolteacher, approaches them. He
tells them his sister works in a pork shop, that she is happy. He
tells them that his English is poor and that he and his parents
live in a single room with a cat. "My parents wish to meet you,
but there are too many people in the street, watching." Muriel
imagines he'd like to slip them into his pocket, like two stolen
cigarette lighters.

That night, the heat remains unabated. It swells in people's rooms. Men and women crouch in doorways, smoking cigarettes. Muriel's sandals make a soft, rubber sound on the pavement. Only one man, stretched on his bed on the sidewalk, snoring, fails to fall silent as she and T walk by. They follow the teacher through a door and up wooden stairs. Small white feathers, pulled from a pigeon's legs, have fallen between the slats. They lie, luminous in the dark. Feet walk along the wooden galleries above.

In the room two chairs, an old man and an old woman stand by the window. "Please sit," they say and smile. Muriel thinks, *I have no right to be here.* She hasn't even learned their language. They will never see her room. The grey cat rubs against her leg. Tea leaves lie in the bottom of her cup. The teacher's mother shows them a photo of him. He is a child. The photo lives in the safety of a drawer. A boy in the street is selling ices from a large wooden box strapped to his shoulder, banging the box with a block and calling, "Ices, delicious ices." The teacher's father carries the ices up the stairs. She sucks the hard, sweet water. All she has to offer is the blood under her skin as she blushes—and her buttocks that prove, as she sits on this chair, that another world exists. Do they want these? She and T are their son's success. They testify to his mastery of a foreign language. She lifts her cup. Tea leaves float in the clear liquid. The air of their city drifts in through the windows. It is gritty with coal smoke and catches in her lungs.

They say goodbye and go out into the street. The tips of cigarettes glow. The buildings lean in the exhausting heat. The narrow street opens onto a square. Tonight, Muriel wonders, will he make love to me?

In the morning the hotel lobby fluffs and preens itself. The larger of its two restaurants has opened its doors. The Russian word *Restoran,* embossed in gold Cyrillic letters on the glass, is only partly covered by a small cardboard sign in English.

"Esther had a cat she called Anna, after Anna Akhmatova the poet," Muriel tells T. "Do you remember the cat last night?"
"Yes."
"Anna was the same pale grey."

A waiter shows them to their table.

"Esther was passionate about the Russian language. My mother fed Anna and changed her litter. She was less successful feeding Esther. You can't imagine the number of cups of tea Esther drank in a day. When I got up at night, to go to the washroom, the light was always on in Esther's room. I was envious of her passion and discipline. Sometimes I'd knock on her door. She'd tell me, 'Don't worry. You'll find what you want to do.' She'd be sitting at her desk with a blanket wrapped around her.

"Out of jealousy I'd urge her to stop working, to go to sleep.

"She started to call my father Medved—which means bear—and Mom, Malenkaya Ptitsa, little bird. Mom signed up for first-year Russian, at the university. She studied for a while but fell behind. It's not an easy language. I don't know how she thought studying Russian would help her understand Esther's refusal to eat. Maybe it was a form of prayer, sitting in her chair repeating, *Apple, pencil, desk* . . . in a foreign language."

Scrolls showing steep mountains shrouded in mist hang on the walls. Bouquets of chopsticks blossom in vases on the large round tables. The waiter brings tea. They don't know what to order.

"Why couldn't Esther have just kept studying Russian?" Muriel asks. "Why didn't it make her happy? She was so good at it." For a month they've eaten only eggplant, green peppers, pork and rice—the four foods T knows the names of. The waiter approaches again.

"I'm not hungry."

"We aren't hungry," T translates.

The sun beats down on the street and the air is still. A boy is selling sweet-bean ices from a box strapped over his shoulder. Muriel imagines the cold sweet ice melting on her tongue and in her throat, but an ice isn't necessary. It would be pleasant and she would only want to buy another. They turn the corner and enter a wide avenue.

The restaurant consists of a large room furnished with wooden benches and tables. On the floor hens totter, pecking at gristle and grains of rice. Customers trickle in and out. Those who can't find seats eat standing. They chew, spit, cough. They talk and call to one another. Cockatoos stripped of their colours. "I want some of that," says T, above the din, and he points at a plate of chicken.

"It won't have any flesh."

"I want the taste."

He guides her to a table as they argue.

"We can't afford it."

"I can."

"What if we can't find work when we get back? We'll have to live in some tiny apartment in a building crammed full of people. It will be as bad as here."

"We'll find work. We can afford to order chicken. What are you afraid of?"

"I've led my life entirely the wrong way. I should have been earning money. I should have listened to my father and studied something practical. When I go back I'll lead a different life. Maybe it's not too late for me to go to school again. I'll study business."

"But you did work, and you have money."

"No, I didn't work. Not really. Only as a waitress, and giving English lessons. Only for a few months. Most of my money my father gave me. And I won't have money if I spend it."

"I'm going to order chicken."

He buys a ticket and hands it to a woman seated behind a low wooden table. She drops the ticket in a bowl of water where the ink loosens. A plate of chicken travels through the kitchen window towards him.

Dearest Dad,

I admired this country. Along city streets they've planted trees. The absence of clutter. The simple clothes. Hong Kong seemed like a harlot, fluttering in frills and sequins. Now I'm ready to leave. They build so many

walls here, to no purpose. Red walls that begin anywhere and end nowhere. I must earn money. You were
so right, money is power. You were right all along. Keep
well.

Love, Muriel

"I want to climb Mt. Emei." Terry runs his hand along his cheek.
As an alternative to shaving with icy water in bustling public
washrooms, he's grown a beard. The train slows inexplicably,
then again picks up speed. "Mt. Emei's less than two hundred
miles from here," he adds.

"Why do you want to climb it?" Muriel lowers her diary.

"They say it's beautiful."

"Who does?"

"The guidebook and Jeremy Pear."

"I wish there were something to drink on this train besides
tea." She drops the shrivelled leaves into her tin cup.

"According to the guidebook foreigners aren't allowed to
climb Mt. Emei. But Jeremy's going, and he's met two Aussie
couples who climbed it without any trouble."

The train has pulled into a village station. Half a dozen
teenagers pile in. Their clothes are ragged. On their backs hang
large open baskets filled with the hard white cocoons of silk-
worms.

"What were the Australians wearing on their feet?" Muriel
enquires. Several of the teenagers have no shoes. She stretches
her arms above her head, her back stiff from hours of immobility.

"Running shoes, I expect. Apparently there are stairs all the
way to the top."

"How many stairs?" The air inside the compartment tastes
hot and stale.

"It took them two days up and one down. I'll take you out
for monkey stew if you'll come. There's a bar at the top. They
serve a beer called Nirvana Light. It's imported from Australia.
Porters carry it up on their backs."

"What do they serve for dessert?"

He cannot stop himself from grinning. "You believe everything I tell you. Don't you?"

Where the face of the mountain steepens, the stone steps shrink to the size of small, hard loaves of bread. The steps appear to have grown out of the mountain. The trees' foliage casts a shawl of shadows over the path. Far below, green ridges undulate. Bony blue fingers stretch. Roots search through stone for water and food. Pilgrims, it is said, once threw themselves from the peak of this holy mountain, into the arms of the Bodhisattva.

Men carry baskets of coal on their backs, sacks of rice and black beans. Some carry aged women whose tiny feet dangle, and whose arms and heads hang limp. Who pays for these porters? Or are they the sons? Beside the path, an old man has spread his medicinal wares on a dirty blanket—mushrooms, roots, and a withered monkey's paw.

"It's not right of him to have killed a monkey," Muriel declares. "My father says Asians don't feel for animals. They work them or eat them. They haven't our understanding of pets. If they do keep one, it's a bird locked in a cage, to be looked at and listened to, nothing more."

"I don't think your father knows what he's talking about. Perhaps Asians understand birds better than he does."

Her father is misinformed. Muriel looks over at T, seated beside her on a stone at the edge of the path. His intelligent blue eyes examine the approaching climbers.

"I've always believed him," she says.

"About Asians and birds?"

"And how the British discovered fair play, and the Christians invented charity."

"You've had a choice."

"At five years old?"

"You haven't been five for a long time."

The air has turned cold. Tatters of mist hang between the trees. Muriel and T have left their heavy knapsacks at the bottom, climbing in cotton shirts and pants, windbreakers tied around their waists. They shiver. "You're right. Five is a long time ago. Will you kiss me now?"

"Later. I'm tired."

"Please."

T presses his lips to her cheek.

Young men and women file past. The women are dressed like schoolgirls in white sun hats and plastic sandals. Large watchbands encircle the men's thin wrists. Old women climb in threes, warm in their padded jackets, the blue cloth bright against the brown skin of their faces and hands. Three who've stopped to rest laugh, smoke, and spit on the path.

"Aren't they beautiful? Look at their leathery skin. I wonder how old they are. And, oh, look; look at that tree."

For a moment Muriel doesn't need to ask, *When will he kiss me?*

In the empty hall of a wooden barracks at the top of the mountain, a brass Buddha tall as two grown men sits cross-legged. Red banners dangle from the ceiling. Young tourists from every province, wrapped in rented army coats, cluster and pose, snap photos of each other with little brown box cameras. *They should all be shot,* Muriel thinks. *They show no respect.*

But if the Buddha is irritated by the commotion, he hides it well. The young people giggle, chatter, shout across the hall. They run along the creaking floorboards. His face wears an expression of dreamy tolerance. His large limbs appear loose, comfortable. A young girl strokes the Buddha's ample thigh; finally a middle-aged man falls prostrate at his brass feet. *Perhaps,* thinks Muriel, *the Buddha is as truly unperturbed by the world around him, as Mom pretends to be. Mom, absorbed by her search for salvation—her salvation and Esther's.*

In the courtyard filled with mist, men crouch, smoking cigarettes, and voices travel disembodied. The sound of feet padding across cobbles comes from every direction and none. Silence. Outside the yard, the milk flows over the top of the mountain, the furthest visible object the charred remains of a tree. Muriel waits for T to find her but he doesn't come. The lighted windows of the barracks float in the milk. She walks back towards them.

T has discovered food, black beans and rice, served in a dining hall. When they've eaten they go to their room. The bed, covered by a damp pink quilt, stands in the corner. A piece of glass is missing from the window, and a small white cloud has floated in. It hangs, caged by the four walls.

He says that Dad is wrong, the Scots not superior. He says that Dad doesn't know.

At dawn they watch the sun rise in a clear sky, above a carpet of valleys and rivers. Then they climb the stairs down the face of the mountain to its feet, where plums and rice grow.

Dear Esther,

T promises that after the Li River we'll head for Macau, Hong Kong, then home. I long to escape this country. When I get home, I'll have to find a way to make money. Should I have studied business? You always know the answers. I'm not sure about me and T. I miss you awfully.

Love, Muriel

They stop in a village on the Li River. In the hotel courtyard stands a round concrete table; beneath it weeds grow in a patch of dirt. A pale English woman in a faded blue and white sundress sits at the table, writing letters.

"I'm catching up on some correspondence," she explains, and laughs. Her teeth are large.

"Have you been here long?" they ask.

"Oh, five days at least. But I don't think a week." Her smile is gentle, tired. They introduce themselves. "Beatrice Brave," she says.

The sun beats down on the dry earth, the weeds and her broad, bony shoulders.

On their third day it rains. The rain begins during the night. Muriel asks T to make love to her, but he refuses. The mosquito net hangs, white and luminous, around his bed. He lies on his back, arms folded under his head. She lifts the net and curls beside him. Mosquitoes press their tiny, dark bodies against the delicate curtain; their sound swells in the still air. Beside the door stand a wooden chair, a small table, and on it a flowered thermos of hot water. "She slashed herself with a razor blade. She licked the blood," says Muriel and he holds her.

Muriel dreams of Esther during the whole of the night. Her childhood swirls like the Li River, flooding the rice fields. The waters rise until they cover the streets. The villagers set out nets to catch fish.

On the fifth day the waters retreat. Muriel and T walk to the market to buy plums—small yellow plums that lie in a basket on the ground. She slips her arm through his. "I love you." It's a sentence she's begun repeating and can't stop. They find a path winding down to the river. The village falls behind a grove of bamboo. The dirt track follows the lip of the embankment. A group of soldiers passes.

"I love you, T."

"I know."

"How do you know?"

"Because you keep telling me."

He smiles and brushes the hair back from her forehead. They peel off their clothes. The brown water glides over Muriel's knees, her navel, and finally her shoulders. As they swim, some men come along the path, talking and laughing, hidden by a thicket. They swim further.

"Is this far enough?" she asks.

"Yes."

They drift back, carried by the current to the rock where their clothes wait. They clamber out.

"You don't love me."

"Yes, I do. Why do you say that?"

"Because you haven't kissed me."

"I was swimming."

"You aren't now."

"It doesn't mean I don't love you."

"There's something wrong with me."

"Maybe," suggests T, "there's something wrong with me."

The sun drinks the water from Muriel's feet, then her legs. It dries her stomach and breasts. Large, hazy clouds hang above the bank, across the river. She rolls over and watches T's chest lower, as his breath escapes. His chest rises, then falls again. His penis rests like a small bird, fallen on its side.

"I hate him."

"Who?"

"My father. And all of you, because none of you wants me."

T lies with his eyes closed, his rusty head resting on his piled clothes. Across the river, the clouds hang above the bank. As they follow the track back to the hotel, dust coats their sandals and toes.

T stands at the foot of his bed. His knapsack has fallen open, releasing a sock onto the floor.

"I want you to make love to me."

"Muriel, I can't. Please stop asking me."

"I've ruined everything."

"You're starting to."

The crook of T's neck smells of sweat and heat, of ginger and coriander. She presses her face into its warmth.

On the sixth day, when they wake it's raining. The water batters the leaves outside the window. T sits on his bed reading. The mosquito coil sends a column of thin blue smoke into the air. Muriel closes her eyes and sees Esther, fourteen, holding a cigarette between her lips, cupping a match in her hand. Muriel walks past Esther, past the painted post that marks the bus stop, her eyes fixed on the building ahead. *I hope you go to hell for this, Esther,* she says, under her breath. *You've lost all respect for Dad.*

The smoke is rising in a column, hanging in the air, thin and blue. "I'm going for a walk." Muriel puts on her straw hat.

T eyes her from the corner of the bed, his book lowered. "It's raining," he warns. She steps out into the wet courtyard.

71

Before Muriel left for China, her mother bought her new socks, a cotton sweater and a hair clip. Her mother provided her with needles, thread and a tiny pair of scissors. Muriel sits in the yard of weeds, at the round concrete table, sewing a tear in her skirt. Beatrice Brave, her paper, pen and address book have climbed the Flying Golden Goose Pavilion at the village's edge to see if they can catch a breeze. T wrings out the laundry, hangs it from a rope stretched between two trees. As Muriel sews, she watches the smooth, taut muscle of his forearm.

"Do you love me?" She tries to ask with a casual curiosity, as if to say, How much were the plums the other day?

"Yes."

"Why don't you tell me?" She hopes her voice sounds light, teasing.

"I do tell you."

"Why don't you tell me every day?"

"Why would my feelings for you change from one day to the next?"

"I don't know. I suppose they wouldn't."

The needle glides through the fabric, out into the air. She pierces the cloth again, the thread following. *Yes,* she thinks, *he does love me. He does, or he would never put up with this.*

She remembers sewing at a table painted a pale green. In the red wing-chair, her gram fans herself, her large, soft body sweating, pressing against the seams of her dress.

"My, but it's hot in here."

Muriel smooths the section of hem she's sewn—"Yes, it's hot, Gram"—and she carries the skirt over for inspection.

"You're doing lovely work, Muriel. But you'll need more bias tape before you're finished." When her gram has hoisted herself to her feet, her warm bulk moves assuredly towards the closet. The shoeboxes are stacked, labelled—snaps, ribbons, lace, bias tape. The closet smells of lavender. Muriel inhales the gentle pleasure of order.

Dear Esther,

The rain has stopped. Yesterday, Beatrice and I borrowed bicycles. Beatrice Brave—an Englishwoman, the only other foreigner staying at our hotel. Well, not our hotel strictly speaking. One day when her brother was a little boy, Beatrice came upon him burying a letter in the soil of the back garden. When she asked him what he was doing, he told her that soon the letter would grow into a parcel. The skin of a plum was caught between my teeth. I stopped pedalling and tore a thorn from a tree beside the road. I was poking between my teeth with the thorn when a man ran from the field waving his fist. His fist held plants he'd pulled from the ground. Damp peanuts dangled amongst their roots. He filled my hands and pockets with the wet nuts. He must have thought I was starving, reduced to eating the thorns off trees. How should I imagine you? Ringing sales into a cash register? Handing books over a counter? I've had a dream you're working in a bookstore. Soon I'll know if this is true. Is it possible, soon I'll see you?

Love, Muriel

For the second time they are trying to leave the village. The first time they bought bread, peanuts and bananas at the market. T found a flat cardboard box to carry the food in. They ran towards the bus then stood cursing as dust covered the bread and bananas, the bus rolling out of sight.

"You must go to Guilin," the short man at the booth told them. He had the faint beginnings of a moustache. He wiped his forehead with a handkerchief. "The bus originates in Guilin, and you must go there to obtain seats."

"We don't want seats." A fly landed on T's arm.

"You must have seats. You are foreigners."

Now a tall young man approaches T and addresses him in English. He is a student from Chengdu, sent here to study the methods of rice harvesting. He removes his spectacles and wipes them with the corner of his sleeve. "There is a bus you can take to Mongian. Mongian is also on the way to Canton." He leads them into the crowded bus bay.

The curious hills of the region rise out of the flat fields, like soldiers dressed in blue. Warm air sweeps through the windows. When Muriel turns, T smiles at her. Two men sit beside him, each holding a covered birdcage on his lap. The road falls like a grey ribbon, too narrow to disturb the countryside. Muriel watches the driver eat tiny yellow plums, spitting the pits through the window onto the road.

When she turns, T is speaking with the men beside him. She remembers that T smiled at her, and she rests her head against the frame of the window. The bus falls, dropping over the crest of a hill.

The bus drives all afternoon. By evening they come to a bluff, overlooking a river. A wooden barge, rowed by eight men, carries them across, the water swirling slowly past, heavy with mud. The town of Mongian watches, crowded on a low grey cliff. Its thin children run down to the shore. The pores of their skin are black with coal from the cooking fires, their clothes rent and frayed.

The children follow Muriel and T through the streets, darting forward like minnows to grab at their pant legs and sleeves.

"Let's go back to the hotel. This is awful," whispers Muriel. They retreat to the asylum of their room. Through the open window come voices and feet, no bicycle bells.

"The only other place there haven't been bicycles was Mt. Emei. I liked Mt. Emei." Perched on the edge of her bed, Muriel wriggles her ankles and toes, drops the dry leaves into her tin cup.

"Jeremy said he wanted to climb a mountain to accustom himself to breathing thin air. He said he was preparing his lungs for law school. Then he lit up a joint. But I shouldn't tell you that. You disapprove of him already."

"No I don't. I quite like him."

"Did you know he could quote Lu Xun in Chinese?"

On the other side of the wall someone coughs, scraping phlegm from their lungs, then spits onto the floor or into a handkerchief, perhaps into a spittoon.

In the morning Muriel and T ride on folding chairs, on the upper deck of a boat. It will carry them to Canton. They watch the drifting clouds. One of the caged birds has died. "It was probably ill when I bought it," says T's friend, and he throws the bird over the railing like a stone. That night they eat, then sleep below in berths the size of coffins, arranged in a row on the floor. There is no room to stand.

In Canton they find a room. Fish are sold from aquariums in the market, puppies from baskets. Bananas lie in mounds on the ground; pastries filled with sweet, red bean paste wait in rows on trestle tables. Muriel tells herself it's not T she loves, but her father. This seems to explain her insatiable longing. T buys them pastries. "I can't manufacture desire," he says.

Yellow and green tiles cover the walls, the ceiling and floor of their room. They've arrived in Macau. There is no window. T stands on one foot, washing the other in the white porcelain sink. They dress with averted eyes. In the street, the sun beats down remorselessly. They order fish and coffee at the New Lisbon Café.

"I wonder what's become of Beatrice," T says, stirring sugar into the lovely strong black coffee. "I hope she hasn't lost her passport again."

Once she left it on the counter of a Beijing bank. Only after the long train ride to Shanghai, when she entered a hotel and reached in her money belt, did her fingers discover its absence.

"We'll probably run into her again. Taste the fish. It's fabulous," urges T.

Men reading newspapers sip their coffee slowly. Empty tables wait patiently. Muriel rests her fork on her empty plate and listens to the blades of the ceiling fan turn, the emptiness a caress.

Late afternoon. They ride on a brilliant green streetcar through the bustling Hong Kong street. Letters have arrived from home—from Esther, from Emily and David. Muriel peers at them excitedly, their weight lovely in her hand. T asks, "Aren't you going to read them?"

"No. I'll wait until after tea."

Stacks of dim sum delicacies lie tempting on a trolley weaving its way towards them.

The first blue letter she slits open was postmarked over two months ago.

Dearest Muriel,

Your letter arrived yesterday. I loved your descriptions of eggplant cooked in a spice that burned, of men and women spitting gristle on the floor. I wonder what you're doing now? Riding in the heat of a crowded train?

Don't give up on "T." That's easy for me to say. I guess what I mean is—are you SURE he doesn't love you? If you can talk with him that's already a lot.

As I explained, at length, in my last letter (Did it reach you?) I've been discharged and am living with Mom and Dad. It's o.k. being at home; but I miss you.

I have a job working part-time at Barrington's bookstore. Since I work upstairs doing orders . . . etc. . . . I don't have to deal with the public, thank God.

Also, I'm going out with a man I met at work (Did I tell you in my letter? How can I not remember?) His name is Chris. He's probably not the sort of person you'd go out with. He's very shy. But I think he's wonderful.

Otherwise I haven't much to tell, except that we've been living wrapped in blankets of hot damp air. Oh, and I made a needlepoint cushion. My break is nearly over (I'm at work). I must go. I love you. Your letters and postcards are wonderful. On the days when I'm at home, as soon as I've heard the postman I hurry to our little milk-box and look for a card or a blue envelope.

Love and a big hug, Esther

P.S. Hello to T.

The ferry crosses to Kowloon. A breeze blows and the water is black. Behind them, coloured lights weave in a crown around the mountain. They walk until they reach the dirty highrise where they've reserved a room.

The New Washington Guest House, an apartment on the fifteenth floor, boasts six small rooms. Three of these are rented to foreigners—African businessmen, passing through, gold watches around their wrists; and white travellers ashamed of their wealth.

A smell of dampness seeps through the wall from the bathroom. The walls are painted turquoise. *Ipsu loves Bilu* is written in pencil beside the bed that fills the room. Just below the ceiling, a small window gazes at the concrete of the adjacent building. Mah-jong pieces clack in the living room. A whisky bottle, filled with drinking water, perspires on the beauty table next to the door.

T lies on his stomach and sleeps, his arm thrown over Muriel's waist. She dreams she is sitting in a room whose walls are the shade of medium green that people choose to paint the corridors of hospitals and dormitory bedrooms. On the desk in front of her, someone's books and a note pad wait to be read. The bed is covered neatly with a brown and red checked blanket. A fashion magazine lies on the foot of the bed. The woman on the cover has eyes like an iguana. She's stitched into a blue dress. Esther enters, from the closet. Her blonde hair hangs to her waist. She is wearing a flowered sundress with straps. It exposes her shoulders and arms. She holds an empty beer bottle in her hand.

"I'm going to break this," she says, and grins.

"Why?"

"So it will be sharp and I can cut myself."

"Won't that hurt?"

Esther stretches on the bed, on her stomach, her feet lifted behind her. She is turning the bottle over in her hands. "Only a little. Not as much as other things."

"What other things?"

"Never mind."

"What other things?"

"Just go away. You don't understand."

Esther takes the bottle by the neck, brings it down hard on the leg of the bed.

On the roof of the YMCA, they order toast and tea with slices of lemon. The waiter, an old man, brings the tea in a white china pot, white cups and saucers, the slices of lemon on a white plate. The entire roof is white, even the low wall. Along the base of the wall, a row of potted plants holds brilliant red flowers.

T is on five down in the crossword of *The New York Times*. Behind the red flowers, behind the white wall, the ferry crosses the blue sky that has fallen into the Pacific and tastes of salt. T is on six across.

"T, I'm going home."

"You don't want to go to Burma?" He speaks slowly, spreading out his words, as though he were laying down pebbles for her to find her way back to him.

"No."

He sets the newspaper on the chair beside him. "I'm not ready to leave yet," he says.

"I have to go. I can't stand this any more."

"Can't stand what?"

She looks into the cup in her hands. "You never want to make love to me."

She hopes he will prevent her from leaving, that he'll press her against the white wall of the roof, among the large, brilliant red flowers, that her limbs will be immobilized.

The rain runs in rivers along the pavement. She closes her umbrella. Her shirt dampens and sticks to her skin. He asks, "Why don't you open your umbrella?" She drags it along the iron rails of the fence. Whackety, whackety, whackety. He holds his umbrella over her.

"I'll never meet anyone else," she says.

"Yes you will," he corrects her.

"You'll never understand how I feel about you."

"Tell me."

The palm of her hand stings his skin in a pink star beside his mouth. Stores up and down the street sell cameras, dirt cheap. Clocks. Gold watches.

Outside the glass window of the bus the air ripples in the heat. The crowd moves in waves under the shop signs that reach out of the buildings, blocking each other from view. Inside the bus the air is cool. Muriel rests her head against the seat. A ramp leads up to the highway.

On the runway the huge metal bird waits on its wheels. Chairs, bedroom suites, parcels of mail, crates of clothing and plastic dolls, and tea fill its belly. Its beak lifts into the air. Muriel leans back in her chair. The steward hands out peanuts in crinkly plastic packets.

T, small as an ant, far below is packing his clothes, she imagines—the balls of socks, his dress pants for crossing borders, his shaving kit. He pays for the room. He shakes hands with the short slender man who owns the guest house. Every night the man loses at mah-jong to his wife. In the late afternoon T will fly in a large metal bird to Rangoon where you can sell a bottle of Johnny Walker Red Label Whisky and live off the proceeds for a week. Muriel closes her eyes. She sees his razor and shaving brush, the loose change from his pocket spread on the beauty table beside the door. His neck smells of coriander and sweat.

The Sun's Hot Examination

Muriel sits on the back steps, watching Esther paint her nails. Already two of the pale ovals are stop sign red. Esther's ripened her eyelids with a plum powder. Her long, blonde lashes bristle with black lacquer. *You're the one who should be leaving. Instead of painting your nails, you could be out looking for somewhere else to live,* Muriel says, but without opening her mouth. The words, crushed into a bitter juice, slip down her throat. *You're older. Why is it always me who has to go away? You have Chris and I don't have T.*

Muriel stands, digging her hands into her pockets. She looks at the narrow stretch of lawn, the wild untrimmed hedge, the patches where the grass refuses to grow in the dirt churned by the dog's paws. Tulips have erupted among the weeds in the flower bed. She thinks, *You're not as weak, Esther, as everyone believes. I won't accept you need lipstick or eye shadow to protect you, or the medication they make you take.*

At the far end of the garden, Muriel notices, Esther has

cleared out all the unwanted stragglers and planted pink and yellow primula. *Today's Saturday. Aren't you going to Chris's? Is he busy?* Esther bends her long, pale neck, applies the last strokes of polish. *Like a swan's neck, Dad says. Do you know how beautiful he thinks you are?*

Why do you never stay the night with Chris? He arrives at the door every evening at seven, and the two of you go for a walk. You walk for hours. Then you stand beside his car in front of the house, and kiss. What are you waiting for? Why don't you move out with him? Why must I be the one to go? You know the four of us can't live here together. I'll keep Mom and Dad company. I might as well, mightn't I? No one comes to collect me at seven.

Esther has screwed the lid on the bottle of polish that sits on the stone step beside her. She holds her fingers open in a fan. Each of her soft, white fingers ends in a hard, red oval. She examines them, looking for streaks or ragged edges, but there are none. She looks up at Muriel and smiles.

Don't you want to move out? The words sit safe inside Esther's mouth. *Me, I'd love to move out. Then Dad couldn't crawl all over me with his eyes. Anything I leave lying around, he reads. When I take my shower, I half expect him to walk into the bathroom, the way he used to, suddenly needing to floss. And the floss was never easy to find. So he could stand as long as he liked, looking for it. I stop washing and listen, in case he's going to appear all blurred on the other side of the frosted glass. Did he do that with you, Muriel? He must have. But if I asked, you'd shrug. Wouldn't you? You'd say, Yeah. I guess it could be scary. It didn't really bother me. He wanted to floss. Let him. That's what you'd say.*

Chris says you'll never see David for who he is. Why should you? David doesn't think of you as a girl. The first time Chris came here to pick me up, he asked if I knew David was looking down my blouse while I weeded the garden.

I asked Chris, So what do you want me to do about it? I was angry, as though he were accusing me of dressing like a slut, of leading Dad on. I don't think there's anything you can do, Chris said. We were sitting in the car, and he drew his hand through his hair. I love his hands. Then he took my hand in his other. He

*said, I know what I'd like to do—punch your father in the face.
Then he started the engine and drove me to his parents' house.
One day, we'll have a house of our own. He says I just have to
be brave and hang on. If we moved out now, we'd lose all our
savings paying rent. He comes for me every day, and we go for
a walk. Do you see why I love him? Do you understand how loyal
he is? You probably don't. You and I are just different, that's all.*
The flow of words inside her has stopped, at last.

Esther admires her nails. They're perfect. Not a blotch. The
cuticles lie flat. The end of each nail curves smoothly. They're
like women's lips in the fifties—vivid but carefully contained.

It's eight o'clock. A civilized hour for dinner, though a little earlier
would have suited David nicely. His wife had trouble deciding
what to make. David Maclaren, his prayer finished, opens his
eyes and tucks his napkin in his shirt. "Well, I think I included
everyone near and dear to me, on my list. Some of those near to
me need more assistance than others. A little prayer can't hurt."

Emily has served the lasagna. Steam rises from an ample
portion on David's plate. When he has sliced a piece and cooled
it with his breath, his daughters take up their knives and forks.
It is delicious, they tell their mother, and she thanks them.

"What have I done to deserve two such beauties for daughters? Not only are they lovely to look at, but they have agreeable
voices."

David looks about him. His family is eating the food he has
provided, and his wife prepared. All is nearly as it should be. But
his daughters are getting older and, if they don't intend to find
husbands, they should be looking for careers. They display a
worrisome disinclination to do either. The lasagna tastes surprisingly good, given he is not fond of pasta. He would suggest to
his wife that she serve pasta less often, but her feelings are
delicate. Tonight the air is cool and earlier he walked briskly
home from the bus stop. The lasagna is settling, warm and
surprisingly satisfying, in his stomach. Perhaps Esther and Muriel
simply haven't any idea what they might be good at. Perhaps it

is not laziness holding them back, but a lack of confidence. He has an idea.

"Either of you two could make a good living reading T.V. commercials," he suggests. "Or, if you're afraid of the camera, you could sell just your voices. I'm sure they're always looking for people with good enunciation to read those books on tape. Though that might take a bit of acting ability as well."

Emily, who at that moment has lifted her fork, lowers it to her plate. "Esther has a job, David. She is working at the Barrington Book Store. And Muriel has just got back from Asia."

Emily, who has never had to support herself, displays a shocking incomprehension of the cost of life. She considers herself to be a woman of imagination. Yet she fails to picture a realistic future for her daughters. Whatever it is she feeds her imagination, it's not the hard facts of survival. Does she have any idea how little Esther's salary will buy? "I was trying to tell these girls what lovely voices they have," David explains patiently. "And that they might use them to make a little money for themselves, that's all. There aren't a lot of women it's a pleasure to listen to in this country, I'm sorry to say. My wife is the exception. I don't know why that's so, but it is."

David slices another piece of his wife's lasagna, lifts a portion of it to his mouth, chews carefully—his mouth closed—then swallows. "What comes out of these girls' throats is a good deal easier to listen to than the stuff that poured out of the woman who came to see me in my office today. She was all in a dither. 'Oh, Professor Maclaren . . .' She didn't understand the assignment, that's why she got it all wrong. 'Well, you could have come to see me before you handed it in, if you knew you were lost, you bimbo.' Of course I didn't say that to her. 'Oh, Professor, it was so difficult . . .' And then she began to cry. The poor woman must have had something else troubling her; the assignment was only worth ten percent of her grade for the year. Perhaps it was her love life. I didn't think she'd appreciate my asking. She might have thought I was a dirty old man. At any rate, I gave her a kleenex. If the whole thing was a performance, she was certainly an accomplished actress, and deserved my admiration. Then, 'Oh, Professor, couldn't you do something about my mark?' There wasn't really anything I could do, short of making up a new assignment especially for her, and maybe averaging the two results. But the truth, I regret to say, is that she'd have got a lot further with me if she hadn't spoken in such a childish whine. Here was a grown woman, fully developed in every way, with a pitiful squeaking voice. She sounded as though she were a little girl trying to wheedle something out of her daddy. I feel sorry for the poor bugger who has to live with her. It was my wife's voice, along with myriad other delights, that attracted me to her. I flew like a bee to honey. And there isn't a day the sweet music of her words doesn't fill my ears."

David serves himself salad, and reflects on what he has just said to his wife and daughters. Certainly, no one can accuse him of lacking gallantry. He pushes the cucumber to one side and begins with some lettuce and a mushroom. Over the years he's developed a taste for salad, by force of exposure. Cucumber he has difficulty digesting. A strip of Esther's lasagna lies unfinished on her plate. He could mention the starving people of the world, but that has never seemed a logical remark given the impossibility of unwanted food on one person's plate reaching a starving mouth elsewhere. Is he to blame for this? He donates money to the Scott Mission and twenty or more other charities. That, at least, is something—more than Esther can hope to do with her salary. If his wife understood this she wouldn't encourage the girls to ignore life's realities.

"Aren't you hungry, Sweetie?" Mrs. Maclaren looks, with a mixture of anger and worry, at the pasta on Esther's plate.

"I've had all I want. It's very good, but I'm full." In her lap, Esther scrunches her napkin into a tight ball.

Muriel forks a large piece of lettuce and a slice of carrot into her mouth.

"You're not eating much either, Muriel," Mrs. Maclaren comments.

"I'm stuffed." Muriel's face has thinned, her collarbone protrudes.

At first Emily thought an Asian parasite might be responsible for the change in Muriel, but the tests have come back negative. What might she have done differently for her daughters? At least they aren't alone. Many young women refuse to eat. Perhaps this collective suffering has even been necessary—a catalyst. Women's strength is rising in a wave that will drown old patriarchal ways. Sometimes Emily can feel this energy out there. Surely some of this collective strength will buoy up Esther and Muriel. It will seep into them.

The dog barks, and Emily gets up quickly from her chair to open the door. For a woman of sixty five she is remarkably agile. Years of yoga have kept her limber. She wipes the mud from the dog's paws, then stroking Tekla's head, offers her a biscuit. "There. Now you go and lie down, Tekla. I don't want to have to wipe your paws twice during dinner." The dog ambles into the living room.

How could I force them to eat? I who loathe being told what to do. I must love them with all my heart.

David wipes the corner of his mouth with his napkin and reflects on his daughters' lack of appetite. It is called *anorexia*. David has read about it on numerous occasions. Women's issues are now considered news. They say most of the afflicted are young women in their teens or twenties. Several culprits are suspected—the fashion industry, demanding parents, and men who don't hold women in high enough esteem. Neither Esther nor Muriel cares much about fashion, as far as he can tell. Certainly not Muriel. Esther, it's true, does cake all that makeup on her face. A pity. As for parental expectations, most of their lives they've been allowed to do pretty much as they pleased. The impact of other men he can't be held responsible for. Their own father is well aware of how valuable women are. Too aware. No. With these girls the culprit (if indeed they are anorexic) is not one mentioned in the articles. Congenital sensitivity. A painful and constant concern with one's own emotions—something he has had to live with and struggle against far longer than either of his daughters has had to. So far, he has felt no need to starve himself.

He takes a kleenex from his pocket, blows his nose and excuses himself. At the opposite end of the table sits Emily. He looks at her and smiles. "You're a beautiful woman," he tells her. "A wonderful cook and the mother of two ravishing, intelligent daughters."

Esther leans her weight against the yellow lawn mower, push-ing it forward. The blades whirr, spitting green slivers of grass into the air. Muriel has come out to read on the steps. Esther, watching her, thinks, *You'll be normal if it kills you. You don't want to move out but you're going to. Every morning I watch you ride off on your red bicycle to find somewhere to live. You bang the metal basket onto the front of your bicycle so violently.*

Yesterday I saw Mom comforting you. You can come home for dinner every day if you like, Sweetie, Mom promised. You'll always be welcome to stay the night. You went over to Mom, where she was standing in front of the stove, and hugged her. You must have wanted her body close to yours. I can't bear it when she touches me. I am the ungrateful daughter. Good will gushes out of Mom, as though I've split her open. It pours, uncontrollably, from everywhere I've wounded her.

Flagstones lead from the patio through the grass to the bed of flowers growing the length of the garage. Esther pushes the yellow mower in front of her. The velvet-capped heads of the poppies bob on their stems, cupped by generous red petals.

The garage is grey, a smaller, simpler replica of the house. Ivy climbs its stucco walls. One night when Esther and Muriel were small, the shingled roof burned as rain fell on a faulty wire. Esther and Muriel sat with their mother on the orange-cushioned living-room bench, watching firemen stomp across the dark lawn, aiming their hoses at the roof in flames at the end of the garden. Emily and Muriel huddled close to their mother, her arms holding them safe.

The blade of the mower catches on a twig and stops. Esther tugs the twig free. *Perhaps I wasn't born into this family. They brought me home from the hospital by mistake, instead of their own child. I've tried to resemble them, but I've failed. I want to watch T.V., and eat popcorn. I wave my hair with a curling iron. Mom watches me and winces, as though the hot iron might slip and touch my skin. Or is she wincing because curling irons are common?*

Muriel has reappeared, carrying on a tray the teapot under

its cosy, two blue and white china cups and a pewter pitcher filled with milk.

"Esther, do you want some tea?" she calls.

"Yes. Please." Esther rests the yellow mower against the oak tree by the hedge.

"What were you reading?" Esther asks, as she sits down on the terrace step.

"*Baltic Nationalism.* It's interesting, but I'm a hopelessly slow reader."

Esther bends her head over her cup. The milky tea has risen to the very rim. One careful sip. Now she lifts her head. "I wouldn't want to read it at all. I think you're courageous," she announces.

Muriel laughs, and examines her shoes. The sole on the left one has come unglued, and the leather has worn thin over her largest toe. The thought of choosing a new pair terrifies her. If the new ones fit with stockings, how will she wear them with socks? Is handsome or durable more important? She doesn't know the answer to either question. Twigs and acorns have fallen on the patio. At her new home there won't be anywhere to sit outside.

Muriel examines Esther. Today Esther has tied her hair back in a ponytail. She's wearing jeans and a small black cardigan she bought at a yard sale. Today her nails are painted a robin's egg blue.

Dad once showed me a robin's egg. Will any man other than T ever love me? T loved me, but I scared him away. The way I frighten Dad, who nudges me with his elbow when I hug him—You're getting too close. Maybe T will write tomorrow. He'll say he misses me. He'll write that he's coming home.

Esther is cradling her cup, her fingers feeding on the warmth. Her broad, red lips sip slowly.

I could never drink that slowly. Esther has patience. She's the one who should be going back to school. "Will you ever go back to school?" Muriel asks.

"I hope not."

"Why not?"

"I'm not interested."

But you can't stay at the bookstore forever. The words bump against Muriel's teeth. *Surely you don't want that? Of the two of us, you were the better student. Brilliant, but an emotional mess. Do I believe that? In a strange way I'd like to. You can't have both—brilliant and stable. What would that leave me?*

The mower whirrs again. Muriel watches her sister push the heavy yellow machine. Esther's lips have left two thick red marks on her teacup. Sometimes now, Muriel wears lipstick herself, and everyone says it suits her. Eye shadow and nail polish are another matter. They lean toward dissolute.

The lawn is silent, Esther standing still at the bottom of the steps. "I've been thinking," she says. "If you need an extra chair—for your apartment—you can have the one with the yellow seat, in my room. I hardly use it, but it's really comfy."

"Can I?"

"Of course. Chris and I also thought you might like help cleaning the windows. Unless you've organized something . . . with friends."

Acorns lie on the stone terrace.

"No, I haven't. That would be great."

Muriel has always had loads of friends, Esther thinks. *This is as it should be. When you're quiet and shy people don't speak to you. Friendships are the reward of the courageous.*

Muriel has gathered the tea things on the tray.

Esther watches Muriel lift the tray easily. *Muriel's long, muscular arms would lift a box of books with the same assurance. And on top of that she's studying Baltic nationalism— politics.*

"I'd like to have someone come and collect me every evening. A man," Muriel remarks. She turns and walks into the porch.

Esther follows. In the back porch, old magazines wait in stacks to be read. She'd like to toss them all out. *If this house were mine I'd seed the lawn, finish weeding the flower beds and hire someone to paint the outside of the house. Chris says the house could be lovely if David and Emily took care of it.*

In the kitchen Esther plugs in the kettle. "If I had a man who loved me, I'd be in heaven," Muriel growls, as she puts down the tray. She glances at the kettle. "Are you having more tea, already?"

There's a hole in the ceiling, cut a year ago when the upstairs bathroom pipes were repaired. Esther looks up at the hole. No one's come to fix it. *Poor father can't afford such luxuries. We're living on the edge of poverty, and don't you forget it. I'm the one holding you back from the abyss. Do as I tell you or I'll let go, and then your incompetent feet will slide. Down the muddy slope. Perhaps Muriel's prehensile toes will find a root to grip. No such hope for my fat feet or Mom's. But the two of us have lovely, soft female forms. Mom's are a little softer than they were twenty years ago. But, oh, she's a beauty still, in the light with the dark behind her. I hate him.*

Esther drops the tea bags into the pot.

And Mom must hate me.

"The likelihood of my ever meeting someone is about nil," Muriel complains. She is sitting on the yellow counter, chewing her fingernail.

"You probably will meet someone. But that's only the start of it. Chris and I have worked hard at our relationship." The tea is not strong enough yet. Esther pours it back into the pot.

"Well," says Muriel, "I don't even have one to work on, do I?"

Esther opens the bathroom door and steps into the narrow, familiar room. She sits on the toilet lid and shakes while a single question reverberates in her head, hammering on the inside of the bone. *What have I done to make you and Mom so jealous?*

As Esther mows the lawn David watches her from his study window. He looked up from his papers and there she was. *We nearly lost you. Who were you doing battle with? Me? Your mother? It isn't easy to fight free of despair. Perhaps you're genetically predisposed. Years ago I saw a snake slip along the wall of a room. Its green tongue was flicking the air. I knew it wasn't really there but I didn't dare touch the wall. I concentrated on the theorem in front of me for as long as I could and when I looked up the snake was gone.*

Whatever your predisposition, that school we sent you to

certainly didn't help. Why in hell they had to give you Sartre to read and Sylvia Plath. Then they introduced you to all those Russians you holed up with.

I saw Sartre interviewed on television shortly before his death. He had a cigarette stuck to his lips, the way most of his fellow Frenchmen do. As though the rest of the world gives a damn how virile they think they are. He said nothing he'd written about life being absurd depressed him in the least. I wanted to pull him out of the television and kick him.

Emily says, "Esther hasn't had any potatoes. Perhaps she doesn't like them?"

She gazes at her daughter's smooth, pale throat and hands. At times it feels irritating to cook food and see it left uneaten. *Do you think it is too much to ask, that you eat my potatoes? If Chris cooked you potatoes, I expect you'd eat them. I've known you much longer than he has. But you treat me as though I'm a stranger. What do you hold against me? Haven't I tried to defend you? Don't you think I saw right away how hard it was going to be for you, for all of us, but for you especially because you were a child and his first? Perhaps I've already told you this. I've never forgotten it. My parents had come to visit us at Christmas. The idea was your father's. I was pregnant with Muriel and my mother's letters showed she was concerned. It was unusual for a woman to have had a first child after the age of forty. Then to be expecting a second, less than two years later. Invite them for Christmas, your father said. They'll see for themselves how wonderful you look. We drove to meet them at the airport, in a snowstorm. I held you on my lap in the front seat. On the return trip my parents filled the back seat. Suddenly something small fell off the car—a hub-cap, I think. Your father stopped on the shoulder of a three-lane highway. He stepped outside. The air was full of blowing snow and the sun had gone down. In the rear-view mirror, I could just make him out as he walked back along the shoulder, looking in the snow for the hub-cap. He left us sitting there, for a hub-cap. I've known ever since I couldn't rely on him in a crisis. He loses all sense of proportion. Every time you made a mistake, he raised his voice. Don't you think I tried to protect you? Who do you think argued with him, late, after you'd gone to bed? All children drop things, David, I'd say. It wasn't a special china cup, I'd tell him. And later, A radio, David. A radio's not going to corrupt her. A little rock 'n' roll. I defended you against everyone I could. When they wanted you to speak in front of the class, I sent a note. I returned shoes and skirts, blouses, bathing suits that didn't fit, that were the wrong colour. Don't you think I tried? Is it too much to ask you to eat two potatoes?*

"I thought you liked potatoes, Esther?"

"I do like potatoes, and I'm about to serve myself some."

"If you don't like them, you don't have to eat them. There's bread in the kitchen."

Muriel and her father drive north. They pass between towering granite walls and over the blue tongues of lakes. Roots grab at scarce soil. Poplar and pine grow tall. Grasses crowd into small pockets. The warm air whips Muriel's hair into her eyes.

"Slow down," David says suddenly. "Pull onto the shoulder." In the ditch a loon is struggling, failing to lift its awkward body into the air.

David has opened the car door.

"Either it's broken its wing," he says, "or that bit of water in the ditch isn't big enough for it to take off."

Muriel can hear, now, the whistle and shiver of the trees in the sun. The bird's black bulk and red eye stare at her. Her father has taken his raincoat from the back seat and is walking towards the loon. When he has dropped the raincoat over the loon he lifts the unwieldy parcel in his arms.

They drive three kilometres further, the bird motionless in the raincoat on David's lap. The rippled blue of a lake appears. "Pull over here, Sweetie. This should do."

When David releases the loon it does not move. Water carries the bird sideways. Then it is running, chest high, wings taut and beating. It has left the water below. "Bravo," her father calls. "We were rooting for you. Good luck."

Muriel pedals through the damp July heat of the late afternoon. She imagines the slender metal door that covers her mail slot. Behind it, a long letter stands on its end. The envelope is addressed in T's hand—closer to print than script, each letter separate but quickly formed. "Dear Muriel, I'm so sick of travelling alone. I miss you enormously. I'm enclosing an address in Jakarta, where I can be reached for the next month. Please, do write. I've been hitchhiking, and the truck drivers here are mad. . . ."

She is cycling up the hill to St. Clair. There is no breeze. The bitter fumes from the cars rub in her throat. *There won't be a letter,* she thinks. The driver of a car, rushing to the beer store, or to a meeting in a restaurant, will fiddle with the knob of his radio. The restaurant has dark, upholstered love-seats. He'll stray into Muriel's path and knock her onto the pavement. She'll wake between clean, crisp sheets on a hospital bed. The corners of the sheets will be tucked carefully, the way her mother taught her to fold them, saying, "These are called hospital corners." The pillow has been patted full of air and settles gently under the weight of her head. The door opens, introducing a tired nurse who holds a thermometer. "It's time you left," the nurse announces. "You've been here long enough. You're the only one who can cure yourself. Don't expect anyone to do it for you."

Muriel stops in front of a low brick building. In the hall she opens her mail slot. No letter. She hoists her bicycle to her shoulder. Carpet covers the first flight of stairs, worn to the thread. The second flight is covered in dark green linoleum. Carmen, the superintendent's wife, washes the halls and stairs daily. Ben, her husband, seated in a folding chair by the front door, sips tea and liquor from a clay mug. In the late afternoon sun he enjoys glasses of pink lemonade and whisky. His skin has a yellow cast. Last week Muriel noticed a bruise on Carmen's cheek. On the fourth floor, one of the glass, triangular lamps has broken and not been replaced.

Though the blind is pulled down over the large window to keep out the heat, light floods Muriel's room. Her mattresses, stacked in the corner, are covered by a Peruvian blanket. She's sewn green and gold corduroy covers for the pillows. At night the taxi driver next door chats with his relatives in Hydrabad. He raises his voice as though air not wires were to carry his voice the immeasurable distance home. To his mother he talks for hours, drunk, apologizing for the same crime over and over, slipping, one foot in Hindi, the other in a pool of English.

Muriel's books cover two wooden planks, balanced on red bricks. These were her father's shelves before her mother bought him proper ones. Hidden behind the boards is an unusable coal-gas fireplace. Its ornate metal pokes up behind the books. Emily's old white and blue teapot stands on the folding table Emily bought for sewing but didn't use and which now is Muriel's. There was more room to spread out pieces of material on the dining-room table.

In Muriel's kitchen, two windows. The east window looks on the back-ends of stores, the south window stares along an alley bordered by trees and fence, up to the roof of a church. Clouds pile behind the steep black roof.

The desk must fit in the kitchen to be out of sight of Muriel's bed. Two books have been left open on the desk, surrounded by floundering notes, ideas clinging to each other, gasping quotations.

Economics—ugh. Politics—ugh. But what the hell else could I have chosen that was serious? If I stick at it, some of the real world will seep into me. Float out my obsessive thoughts about myself.

Muriel washes a plum and sits down at her desk. She imagines she's standing in an auditorium. The students, pens poised, wait for her lecture to begin. She intends to speak on Robespierre but can't remember the date he first came to power, only that his father was a butcher . . . or was that Danton's father? The students rustle their papers. "Tell us the date he came to power," someone shouts. They rap their rulers on their desks. A whistle. A crumpled sheet of paper lands at her feet. Muriel puts down her plum. A wad of the notes on her desk crumples easily into a ball. She tosses the ball into the wastebasket, then retrieves and unfolds it. She starts to cry but stops herself. She inhales a large breath of air. Exhales. Inhales another.

Who were these men? What made some fight arduous verbal battles to keep Siberia, while others regarded it as a wasteland, too expensive to administer?

Muriel has felled quotations that lie across the page, too large to move. But none of them tells her what she wants to know. Did the grandmothers of these men serve them tea in large, cold living rooms? Did they have maiden aunts? There must have been something tiny to begin with, something still folded in on itself. Then it opened its petals and became Russia's Siberian Policy of the seventeenth century. The petals wilted and fell, leaving a musty fragrance. Did a maiden aunt sweep them up? There was no glacial force—economics, or history—rolling forward, depositing gritty policy in mounds, here and there. The beginning was someone's aunt, sitting on a hard chair, with a lump of sugar in her mouth, lifting a glass of tea to her lips. A thousand such aunts transmuted into policy, as did the fathers wearing furs (from Siberia?) tramping down the steps to their waiting sleigh and serf, the sound of bells, the pout the father's lover made, her face next to the glass window, looking down into the street to see why he was late. These all add up, admittedly, to a crowd, a demand for a supply of furs, but why must the individuals in that human mass disappear?

Muriel cuts sections from her notes, glues them onto new territory. The image of Siberia as a rose, black from the cold, is growing in her mind.

The October leaves have turned from green to gold and mauve. A blue sky squeezes between the roofs of the houses. The morning air stings Muriel's lungs, crisp and cold. A young man has fallen in love with Muriel. He fell the day she reprimanded him in defence of a stone and a tree. They were walking in the woods, and the stone—an ordinary, if somewhat large, grey stone—sat nestled among the roots of a toppled tree. He pulled it out. "Don't," she exclaimed. "That stone belongs to the tree." He saw she was right and he returned the stone. He saw that for her the smallest violent action was dangerous, that she understood nature must be left alone. At that moment, he longed to kiss her. He leaned forward, the tiniest bit. She walked on ahead. Later that afternoon, as he lay in the grass, his eyes closed, something delicate but sharp touched his cheek. As he looked up, he spotted a blade of grass in Muriel's hand and knew that she liked him. On their walk back to the road he stopped her and kissed her.

When he left Thunder Bay, not knowing where he'd live next, he stored his possessions in a friend's house. Now Muriel drives with him into the winter's first snow. She helps him load his furniture and belongings into his truck. "This is the first time," he confides, "anyone's ever helped me to move." He holds her hand.

He has found himself an apartment in Toronto. As they wash the walls they argue because, he says, of the fumes from the cleaning liquid. He empties the pail and opens the window, letting in cold fresh air. "We'll use soap and water."

He's come to take her out to dinner. She criticizes his grammar and asks why he doesn't work for a larger, more prestigious paper. "Why do you choose to work freelance, instead of at a full-time job?" At times like this he wonders if she still likes him. He rolls down the truck window and lets in cold, fresh air. Before they reach the restaurant she's become tender and funny. Her questions always make him think. Though he's thin as a rail, at night she pinches his waist, to see if he's getting fat.

One evening near the end of November, he comes to her apartment to take her to a film. He is wearing his winter coat. "I can't go with you. This is all too much. It has to end," she tells him. He leaves in a rage. An hour later, he wonders if it was his coat she didn't like. His rage having frightened him, he decides she needs tenderness. He has bought a bouquet of flowers and knocks on the small, dark door of her apartment. Though she lets him in, her mind is made up.

"I haven't the courage. I can't bear the strength of your feelings for me." Her face has become hard and stern, but a soft light is falling from the lamp on her hair. He sits on the floor, beside her mattresses, and cries. After some time, his mind clears. He looks up and accuses her of being a revisionist.

"You think," he tells her, "you can erase what we've lived through this past month, because the reality of it makes you uncomfortable, but you can't. You've loved me, and nothing you say or do can change that. I won't let you get away with this."

After he's left Muriel collapses on her bed, her face hidden in her pillow. Over the months that follow, he writes to her once a week. He loved her intensely, he says. He sends an article on Elizabeth Smart, who admits to having a sliver of glass in her heart. His work is progressing, he says, his contacts increasing, and his articles fetching a better price. His letters arrive less frequently. He's applied successfully for a job in Montreal, and soon will be moving. They meet for coffee. Then he has left the city.

Muriel cycles down the Bathurst Street hill to her classes, and home in the afternoon. Her paper, considered well researched but confusing, receives an adequate mark. She has received a letter from T. He is in Toronto and seeing a Canadian woman he met in Jakarta. He includes a photo of Muriel standing beside him on the top of a Chinese mountain. She is scowling, wrapped in a rented army coat. The coat is heavy and damp and hangs below her knees. Tatters of white mist drift about them. She writes an exam on the causes—economic, social and intellectual—of the French revolution. Another on tsarist administrative policy in the seventeenth century. Most evenings she keeps busy, visiting friends. Fridays she sits in a darkened cinema watching and listening to someone's life unfold in front of her, ı a screen. Generally, there are many men in the seats near ers. Before and after the film, she looks at them, imagining she ıas the courage to ask them to drink a coffee with her. If she did, who would stop her from destroying them?

The loaves of rye are long and smooth and sit on the top shelf. On the second shelf lie the whole wheat, swollen. Others are square; beside these the seven-grain, the domed cornmeal, the Italian white with cracks in their hard crusts. Muriel tries to imagine the insides of the loaves, whether they are moist or dry, heavy or light. The salesgirl's attention shifts from the seeds on the counter to Muriel's face. The girl smiles. Muriel has read, somewhere, rye is healthiest—less likely to cause cancer of the colon. But another article praised whole wheat—the only grain to stave off Alzheimer's disease. There are bagels mounded in a large bin.

"How much are those?"

A dollar twenty will only buy three, whereas one dollar and seventy-five cents is the cost of a whole loaf of rye. But she wants a bagel. A bagel is complete, not merely a slice of something. Muriel orders two bagels. The salesgirl lifts them with tongs into a small plastic bag. Poppy seeds fall on the counter. Muriel wonders if this choosing bagels will become a habit. This small indulgence could lead to earrings, silk scarves, shoes. The salesgirl enters the item on the cash register.

"I'm sorry, but could I have a loaf of dark rye instead? I'm so sorry." Muriel pulls out her wallet and searches for the exact change. She finds the right coins and puts them on the counter.

Muriel sits down on the cold sidewalk, the loaf of rye resting solid and dark on her knees. She imagines cutting a bagel in half, the two soft, pale circles, the smell as they warm in the toaster. She stares at the odious loaf of rye. *What if I want to make French toast? Rye will be useless. You fool, why did you choose this loaf? Can't you think? Yes, I can. I can so think. I'll show you. Wait till I have my master's in history, then you'll have to believe me. Won't you? Answer me, won't you. God damn you.*

Don't swear at your father. David's voice comes from inside her.

I'm sorry.

In my day, a gentleman didn't blaspheme in front of a lady, and a young lady was certainly expected to keep her language pure.

I'm sorry.

The road to hell is paved with good intentions.

I'm sorry, honestly. I didn't think.

Why did you buy the rye, if that's not what you wanted?

I don't know.

Well, perhaps you'll have learned something.

I have. I do learn. I learn all the time.

That's good. That's my Sweetie.

Dad? Why is Esther always so sad?

She didn't use to be, when she was little. What a smile. You probably don't remember. You'd have been too small. God, what a gorgeous smile, under those blue eyes of hers. I used to feel sick, wondering how she'd look after herself.

Why?

The world isn't always a safe place for a beautiful young girl.

Dad. Why is Esther so sad?

I don't know. Perhaps it was the way I raised her, though I did the best I could.

Dad. Am I a failure?

Oh, Muriel. You could be a success at anything you put your mind to. Don't you know that? That's what I've always told you.

But am I a failure?

I know what you're suffering. I've often felt like a failure myself. The worst was a long time ago—long before you were born, or even thought of. I was sixteen and sitting the provincial scholarship exams. In those days everyone had to sit what was called the Senior Matric. The bright boys went on to compete for scholarships. I'd come out of the room early, and was feeling quite pleased with myself. I thought I'd wait and see what some of the other fellows had to say; and I was curious who would finish next. After a while the boys started filing out in pairs and threes. They stood about in the hall, comparing their answers, and as I listened I felt a horrible feeling in my stomach. For three of the most important questions, not one of them had the same answer as mine. I walked outside, and onto St. George Street. Perhaps I was thinking how, eventually, it led down to the lake, or in that direction; I had the notion of throwing myself in. At any rate, I kept walking all afternoon, with that same, terrible churning in my stomach.

And then what?

I took the bus home, I suppose. The subway wasn't built then.

And then? You did win a scholarship, didn't you?

Oh, yes. Two, and I had to choose between them. But that part wasn't difficult.

What about me, Dad?

You'll feel a good deal happier, the less you think about yourself.

What should I think about?

You might try reflecting on the planet. It's in a hell of a mess, and could use some kind thoughts.

I do worry about the planet.

Not worry—kind thoughts, the sort your mama says will heal things. Or you could try, as I've often suggested, thinking about people less fortunate than yourself.

What do you think about, Dad?

Mostly words and numbers.

What do you think about them?

I play with them. I'll give you an example. *Snug llamas loot tools, a mall, guns.* Lovely and simple. It reads the same way backwards or forwards, a palindrome. It took me a while to think of that one.

The last light touches the fronts of the shops. Its warmth bathes the pavement. The loaf of rye bread sits complacently on Muriel's knees.

"Do you know what time it is, please?" Muriel asks a woman walking past.

The woman doesn't speak English. She smiles, shaking her head in confusion.

"Ten past six," offers a woman in a green wool hat. Plastic shopping bags hang from her hand. She has thin lips and small dark eyes. Muriel stuffs the loaf of rye under her arm and walks to the subway. The sun has sunk even lower, spreading its pink in a blush across the sky.

The subway car jolts and grinds from stop to stop. Muriel sits on the smooth grey-blue vinyl bench. She wishes her mother were beside her. Outside the window the black wall of the tunnel rushes past.

"Mom?" The Peruvian blanket feels soft under Muriel's cheek. Her toes touch the end of the mattress.

"Yes, Sweetheart." Emily has brought cookies and tangerines. Tea has brewed in the familiar old blue and white pot. As Emily shifts position and the director's chair creaks, she wonders if the old canvas will hold her weight.

"What makes Esther so unhappy?"

"I don't know."

"Why are we so different?"

"Even as babies you were. Esther would lie peacefully against my chest, whereas you wriggled and squirmed."

"Was I an awful baby?" Muriel sits up.

"No. You were a lovely baby. But you had colic and that made you cry."

"Did Esther cry?"

"Not much. She was very quiet."

"Dad says she had a beautiful smile."

In the alley, outside the window, a car's tires press into the gravel. From the next room comes a frenetic Bombay musical, a jungle of gyrating mango-shaped breast.

"Yes. Esther had a lovely smile. It's still lovely." Emily takes a cookie. "My last one. You've hardly had any, Sweetie."

"I've had several. So, Esther was cheerful?"

"Mostly she was serious. Even with her dolls. She'd line them up on a blanket, in order of size, then spend hours straightening their hair and their clothes, completely absorbed by what she was doing. I envied her power of concentration."

"Do you remember her laughing?"

"Oh, yes. The day she got her first pair of shoes. They were white, made of leather, with laces. She held her feet out the car window and called to a man passing by, 'New boots, new boots.' She laughed and laughed, and she kept calling after him, 'new boots.' "

"And then what happened?"

"How did she become troubled, do you mean?"

"Yeah."

"I don't know."

No more mango-shaped breasts from next door. Three men are repairing the church roof at the end of the alley. The men move, dark and thin as paper against the sky, the large roof sloping away from the ridge where their feet balance.

"Perhaps Esther frightens easily because there's so much in the world I'm afraid to look at."

"Mom. Could you balance on a roof?"

"No, Sweetheart. I don't even like to climb a kitchen ladder."

"Am I a failure?"

"No, Sweetheart. You aren't."

"What am I good at?"

"You paint and draw wonderfully."

"Anyone can." Muriel has walked across the room and refilled her cup from the blue and white pot in front of her mother. "More?" she asks.

"No more for me. And no, not anyone can paint or draw. You do both better than I do."

"Mom. I don't. You're a good artist."

In the dream Muriel has tumbled from a truck. To escape three armed men she's swum across a river, crawled to the door of a car. The driver, a woman, takes her in. She agrees to deliver Muriel to the city. "Do you have money?" the woman asks. "You'll need money for the train when you get there." But suddenly the woman has changed her mind. She is driving off the road, into a field. In the field a house is burning. It is a small house, doll size. Muriel enters a room where naked, plump women dance, trailing gauze veils through the air. A gladiator opens the door and says politely to Muriel, "Follow me." Outside, Esther is waiting. "Don't worry. It won't hurt," she reassures. In the centre of the paved yard stands a crate. Muriel kneels in front of the crate. She rests her head. She waits. When she does not feel the gladiator's sword slice through her neck she opens her eyes. Instead of his sword he is holding a twisted and rusty scrap of metal in his hand.

This is not the dream that frightens Muriel. The sword has shrivelled. The dream that scares her is filled by her mother's face. An immense face. An open mouth. No teeth, no tongue. From that dream she wakes, hot and shaken.

David, Emily and their daughter Muriel drive out of the city on Highway 401. David's briefcase balances on his lap, a cryptic crossword resting on its smooth, hard surface. Because his wife prefers to drive, he has relinquished the privilege with only a modicum of regret. Though he might choose to feel insulted, he has decided not to. More time to work on his puzzles is a blessing. His elder daughter, Esther, has opted to remain in the city and breathe foul air—which is not a blessing. His wife negotiates the turn expertly, tense but not as tense as she'd be were the steering wheel in anyone else's hands. They roll north along the 427.

There is something peculiar about Esther's devotion to her young man. Why don't they marry? Is Chris waiting until he's advanced far enough in his career to support her in style? Hardly. He harbours thoughts of quitting his low-paying job to stay home and sculpt. The young man will encounter disappointment, if he expects to feed off his wealthy father-in-law-to-be.

As they descend into the Hockley Valley, David holds his pencil and puzzle in place. They would like to roll off his briefcase. Cedars cluster along a stream beside the road. The car labours dutifully up the hill, and the fields roll beneath the luxuriant sky. None of this beauty means a damn thing to Esther. Or so it would appear. David takes a chocolate bar from his briefcase. Semisweet, with almonds and raisins. Yum, yum. First he opens the green and yellow paper with the picture on it, then he peels aside the thin foil. He breaks off four squares and, reaching behind him, offers two to Muriel.

"Thank you, Dad."

He is slipping towards the temptation of comparing his two daughters. This is Esther's doing. If she weren't indifferent to the natural world, the countryside she's fortunate enough to live near, he wouldn't find himself comparing her unfavourably to Muriel. Happily there is a solution. To re-establish a balance in the equation, he only has to enumerate a few of Muriel's lesser qualities—her tempestuousness, her lack of verbal restraint. His paternal affections are once more fairly distributed between his daughters.

The chocolate melts soothingly on his tongue. To the right, rows of pine march across a field. To the left an unused pasture flies by. Grasses bend and the last of the Queen Anne's lace floats. They pass a ruffled expanse of green alfalfa. Behind it, the fields are neatly combed, the hay gathered in rolls. Dark, clear shadows lie on the yellow stubble. The blue sky sprawls. A calm close to happiness settles inside him. Then come the maples. For half a mile maples grow along the shoulder of the road, their leaves withered. Their roots are being shaken by the traffic. They've been attacked by last winter's salt. *I'll watch them die,* he thinks.

His wife parks rather far from the house, afraid that if it rains, the wheels will stick in the mud. He comments on the unlikelihood of rain, but quickly retreats from his position, hearing the anger in his wife's voice. "Your mother's a fierce woman to do battle with," he tells Muriel, returning his puzzle and pencil to his briefcase.

"Mom?"

"Yes."

"Tell me about the time Mrs. James phoned from school, all worried about Esther."

The purple leaves of the ash are strewn on the grass. They crunch and rustle, no matter how lightly Emily tries to walk.

"That was a long time ago."

"Tell me anyway."

The slender trunks stand close together like hairs on a giant scalp. They end at the bottom of the hill. Gnarled apple trees grow along the fence. A cloud, thin as teased wool, veils the sky above the marsh.

"She phoned to tell me they'd found Esther asleep under a staircase in the school. She should have been in class. It had happened several times and a few of her teachers were concerned."

"What did you say?"

"I don't remember. Mrs. James asked if Esther was eating well and sleeping at regular hours."

"Was she?"

"I don't know. She looked tired. I was terribly worried. I'd spoken to her, but she'd got angry with me."

"Why didn't you take her to see someone?"

"I guess I should have. But who would I have gone to? Psychiatrists, then, were for the mentally ill. I didn't know where to begin."

"Why was she sleeping like that? Under the stairs."

Grasses grow as tall as Emily's shoulder, next to the stone wall—all that remains of the barn. The stones are of various shapes, collected from the fields. Some are smooth as the skin on her palm, others rough as sandpaper. They've caught the pinks and greys of a sunset, held them longer than human history. Burdocks abound, groundhog holes, and thistles. Deadly nightshade has draped itself on the end of the wall. There is a colourless nest perched in the safety of a thorn tree.

"I don't know why she slept there." Emily turns to look at

Muriel. "Mrs. James also told me she'd seen Esther drinking coffee with the janitor, in his room. It hadn't happened only once. You must have known Mr. Selby?"

"He seemed nice enough. I never really spoke with him. I remember seeing Esther drinking coffee with him, and thinking how stupid she was. Not because he was dangerous, but inappropriate. The only reason I could think of for her going there was that she wanted to show she was different from the rest of us, more adult. Once, as the bell rang at the end of recess, she behaved as though she hadn't heard it. I asked her if she was coming. She said she had chemistry, she hated chemistry and she wasn't going. It was a waste of time. *A lot you know about a waste of time,* I thought, *drinking coffee in a poky room with an old guy who hasn't even been to university.* I wasn't very sympathetic, as you can tell."

Blackbirds land among the bulrushes.

"I felt I had to ask her about Mr. Selby." Emily stops. She takes her lipstick from her pocket. "This must look silly. But my lips get so dry. Even if she didn't want me to I had to ask. Mr. Selby was nice to her, she said, nicer than her friends. They only cared about marks and were intent on proving how smart they were. Like your father, she said. The other girls had their own friends and didn't need her. She asked to change schools. I was afraid she'd be more lonely in a larger, impersonal school. She didn't ask again."

The vivid red patch on a blackbird's wing flashes. Muriel has broken off the head of a bulrush. She holds it in her hand, uncertain what to do with it.

"Mom, tell me something funny."

"I can't think of anything funny. Not right now."

"Tell about your wedding, and Uncle Geoffrey."

"Do you want to hear that again?"

"I don't remember it."

"I was in one of the upstairs bedrooms in the farmhouse on the hill your grandparents owned. It was my parents' room, because there was a full-length mirror on the inside of the closet door, and I wanted to see if my dress was hanging properly and wasn't creased."

"What was the house like?"

"There were ten fireplaces in that house, one in each room, downstairs and up. It was beautiful, but really too large. My father didn't like the country and so it wasn't much used, and then when your aunt and uncle lived there, they had to keep so many rooms closed to keep warm. Their children were young, and all the lovely things Gram had collected to decorate her house with had to be put away. She'd arrive on a weekend with friends, and find the house smelled of diapers. Toys were thrown all over the floor. It didn't really work out for any of them."

More gnarled apple trees grow on the slope of the hill. Green pears hang small and hard from a tree beside the path.

"Were they still living there when you got married?"

"No. They'd bought a farm of their own. Near Parnell."

"What about your dress?"

"I'd put on my dress and it looked fine; then I went to the window. There was a tall man—your father—wandering about the lawn, taking photographs. What on earth was he thinking, walking about with his camera a few minutes before I was to come down, and the minister waiting for him, by the stone wall? I must have called to him, or maybe someone else said something, because he turned and I saw he wasn't your father at all. I'd never met your Uncle Geoffrey, and the back of his head is the same as your father's. That was when I realized I hardly knew your father. I'd looked at parts of him so hard they'd become familiar. I could close my eyes and see the back of his head, or the back of his hands. But I was marrying a stranger."

"But he was a nice stranger, wasn't he, Mom?"

"Of course he was. Very nice."

"Did you go on a honeymoon?"

"Yes. We drove back to Toronto through Quebec. All up the coast of the Gaspé. I loved being near the sea. The sea has a smell."

"What did you do?"

"We drove and we stayed in little motels. Once David pretended he was a character from some T.V. show. He stretched his vowels, speaking very slowly and as though he weren't too bright, a record spinning at the wrong speed. My hands turned clammy. I sat on them to warm them and so that he wouldn't see how damp they were. My God, I thought, am I going to spend the rest of my life listening to this half-wit? He wouldn't stop. I wondered if this slow man was who I'd married."

"And then what?"

"Oh, he did stop, at last. Really we had a very good time. In one motel there was a couple next door who fought. Eventually, one of them must have sat down on the bed, because the springs squeaked, and she said to him, in her lovely, lilting Scottish accent, 'You take me away for a night and a day and you won't even buy me a cupper.' After that your father said, every time he brought me tea, 'Here's your cupper, and am I ever glad I've taken you away for a night and a day.' "

Slender young trees march like flames across the field. Across the stream, a woods climbs the hill. It forms a tall wall that crumbles as the wind reaches through its branches. Crows flap out of the shuddering leaves; the short days of winter in their wings.

"Mom?"

"Yes."

"Do you remember the time Esther threw herself in front of the subway?"

"Of course I do."

"What did the policeman say when he called?"

"He asked if I was Mrs. Emily Maclaren, and I said I was. Then he told me Esther was all right. Someone had pulled the alarm or the driver had seen her. He wasn't clear about that. The train slowed down but passed over her. She was lying with her arms along her sides, and they pulled her out unhurt."

"He told you all that?"

"I think so. I don't remember. He told me she wasn't hurt, that they'd pulled her out, that she'd jumped."

"How did she get to the subway?"

"Don't you know all this, Muriel?"

"Yeah. But tell me again."

"She walked. No one in the hospital said a thing when she left. She went out the door wearing her pyjamas."

"I remember when you called. I had an essay due the next

day. It was my final year and in a month I was leaving for Asia. At that moment I hated her. I'd been to visit her the day before. I thought, why did I bother? She was going to try and kill herself anyway."

"They'd put her on a new medication. The side effects weren't the ones they'd expected or given her anything for. The side effects were horrible, first everything outside shaking, then the same shaking inside. She told me that's what she couldn't stand any more."

"Do you believe that's why she jumped?"

"Don't you? Has she told you something else?"

"No. Nothing."

Emily sits on a fallen beech tree. "I feel short of breath, that's all." The maples have grown dense and tall. Emily follows her daughter into the yellow leaves, whose fragile cells brim with light. A wire fence marks the end of the property. It passes through the middle of a tree, then collapses where the posts have toppled.

Muriel's foot descends on the pedal. She gazes at the silently revolving tire. Black pavement fleeing. The squat brick storefronts. People and trees are running. Wooden poles hold out the names of streets. The thick heat collects between her shoulder blades.

Muriel leans her bicycle against the window of a hat shop. She curls on her side on the sidewalk to rest. The woman from the hat shop crouches, holding a glass of water. On every corner a thin young woman is standing, a razor blade in her hand.

The taxi delivers Muriel and her bicycle to a friend's apartment. On the other side of the blind, people walk along the sidewalk. Muriel's head rests on the pillow and the blanket's silk border touches her chin. In the early afternoon of the following day she sits on her friend's back stairs. Behind a fence someone moves a car. Two women are talking, too far off for her to understand what they're saying. They're young. Even the sun is young. It pops up every morning, as though no one told it what happens during the night: Nothing but dead stars. She bangs her head against the frame of the door. There's a hole in memory burned by the sun. I've been searching too long and my wings have come apart, their wax melting. The earth is coming up hard and flat.

She rests her head on a pillow of soft feathers.

"Can I help, Dad?"

"You can hold back this branch while I clip under here. I want to get the blades . . . in there. Beautiful. Thank you."

Muriel lets go of the branch and the thorn tree falls on its side, small and slender. She tosses it out of the path into the deep grass.

"Is that o.k. or is there a particular spot you want it?"

"Over there's where I've been putting them." Her father points to the branches he's piled beside the stones, where no one is likely to walk. He loosens the scarf around his neck. "I thought it was going to be colder than this."

They climb further up the hill. He shows her where the new path will turn, the stones he's fitted in the opening of a ground-hog's hole so the tires of his tractor won't catch.

"Groundhogs have plenty of holes. I don't expect they'll miss this one."

The new path will enter uncharted territory. There's consid-erable clipping to be done in preparation, he explains. The path will curve at the edge of the beech woods, and if you stop there and look down, you'll see the stream where it slips between two poplars.

She waits while he clips a branch. He's stopped now, and looks out over the valley. He is seventy years old, his rounded shoulders hide his chest. His stomach is hard and flat. His cheeks have a high colour, as though recently scrubbed clean. His grey hair grows thick. He hasn't trimmed his moustache and a few hairs hang over his lip. His eyes, set deep in their sockets, shine dark and bright.

"One evening as I sat at my desk, attempting to work through the complex implications of a table of interest rates, I failed to make any progress. I couldn't rid my mind of the image of a young man having his way with Esther." A branch has caught David's attention. He snips it, then lets his arms rest, the shears dangling from his hands. "I'm telling you this, because you've been asking about Esther. Rather persistently, I might add. At any rate, I couldn't rid my mind of this image of a young man having his way with your sister. I looked out at the backyard. There was the young man. Your sister sat in a wicker chair. She was wearing a sundress that exposed her arms and shoulders. The young man could see how soft her skin was. Then she lay, in that way she has—limp and boneless, on a bed. The dream—I must call it that I suppose, though I was most certainly awake, had changed location abruptly, as dreams often do. The young man seemed angered by her lethargy. He wanted to see her move, and he pulled her legs apart. He peered inside her, then penetrated her with his fingers, exploring the curious folds and formations. She began to giggle. He thrust himself inside her. He filled her with himself. He hammered her with his body. When he rolled onto his back he was spent. She made no attempt to move. The room seemed to him large and empty. The plaster was spread white and flat on the ceiling. He kissed her and she turned her head away. He pulled her and she flopped onto her stomach. He entered her from behind, like an animal, his cock thrust inside her. She lay perfectly motionless.

"When I couldn't stand these images any longer, I got up from my desk and went to your sister's room. I knocked at her door, but she didn't answer. Her own father had no right to enter. I knocked more loudly and shouted to her through the door that I must speak with her immediately, that I was her father. I told her I loved her. And then, I cried. She stood in front of me, barely seventeen, wrapped in a red dressing gown. Her eyes were even larger and more blue than I remembered. Her neck was long and pale. The soft skin of her throat and chest disappeared beneath the folds of her nightgown. Every man, every Tom, Dick and Harry who passed her in the street would want to touch her, couldn't help himself from wanting to. I told her she had to be careful, that she reminded me of a woman I once desired passionately, a beautiful blonde, not your mother, a woman I never possessed. 'You'll do that to men,' I warned her. I'd taken a tissue from my shirt pocket and wiped my eyes, then I blew my nose. But I began to cry again. I'd thought if I warned her it would help, but still I could only see the powerful danger she faced. When I reached to put my arms around her, she recoiled. I'd risked everything to come and warn her, to tell her how I felt, and she wouldn't let me touch her. 'My God, don't you see I love you?' There was nothing else I could say, my hands were trembling; I turned and left her room.

"In the days that followed, she avoided me. I realized she'd never loved me, never wanted me as her father. I remembered how, when she was a child, her eyes would fix on something invisible that led her into a dream where I was not invited to follow. After our encounter, she became more self-absorbed than ever. She spent entire days shut in her room, listening to mindless pop music. When she emerged, she pecked at the sumptuous meals your mother had gone to pains to prepare. She closed herself off to everything your mother and I had tried to teach her over the years, and opened herself like a sponge to the opinions of strangers. When I think about it, what hurts the most is the waste of her intelligence. She could have been a success in any number of careers. And her failures are of course Daddy's fault. Everything these days is the fault of some man. Apparently I'm a lecherous old sot, but just don't know it. God, if she knew how I love her." David covers his face with his hands.

A fat cloud has strayed into the sky. The trees have nearly all lost their leaves, exposing the land's hips and thighs, the swollen curves of the earth covered in grass and the deep grooves. Muriel's father clips another thorn tree and carries it to the pile. Then he turns to look at Muriel. "I get quite excited about these paths, and then I wonder who will maintain them. Your future brother-in-law's not much interested in the out-of-doors. Nor does your sister appear to be. Maybe that's what keeps them together, a mutual dislike of the country. I suppose they find each other interesting. They certainly spend a good deal of time talking together. Perhaps Chris has a lot to say. He reads the paper. Your sister reads, but she doesn't care to tell me what. I should make these paths because I love to, your mother says, not for anyone else who then feels obliged to enjoy them. Well, I can assure you I didn't buy this place to oblige anyone to like it. I bought these woods and fields for myself, for the pleasure of protecting them and watching them change. If any of you enjoys walking in them, more power to you. I don't intend to lose any sleep worrying whether or not I'm making my family happy by providing them with somewhere beautiful to retreat to in the country."

"What's the next path you have planned, Dad?" The question lies in Muriel's palm. She offers it to her father, holding her hand flat and still. The next path will wind up and over the Big Hill. It will pass under the branches of a large birch and into the back field. To walk along the path will be easy, the shorn grass obedient beneath her feet.

Each page is marked by a circled number on the upper right-hand corner. Arrows snake in myriad directions, shuffling paragraphs and sentences. The pages that won't fit on Muriel's desk she's stacked on the floor. Outside the window a car drives down the alley, gravel crunching under its tires. Muriel gathers an armful of papers and drops them in the wastebasket. The basket fills quickly. She brings a large green garbage bag from the kitchen and continues gathering wads of notes, drafts of chapters.

When every paper is out of sight and the large green plastic bag twisted shut, she pulls a blue sheet of letter paper from the folder on her dresser and writes:

"Why did you hurt us? Not just Esther, but me. Didn't you have any idea how your words made us feel? And have you changed? What was Esther supposed to think when you turned up at her bedroom door, crying and telling her about some woman you'd had the hots for? You're the thinker. Why didn't you think about her feelings? Fuck you. Fuck. Fuck. Fuck . . ."

She slips the folded letter into an envelope she addresses to her father. *I'll finish it later.* The blue envelope lies on the table looking up at her.

She carries the large green bag of essay notes and drafts out of the apartment, and down the back stairs to the cans in the alley. A woman passes, leading a child by the hand. A man opens the back door of his store and sweeps dirt and candy wrappers, some used kleenex onto the square of pavement where he's parked his van. Muriel buttons her sweater against the cold, raw air. She hurries indoors and up the back stairs, two at a time.

Through the window she continues to watch the alley, but the flurry of activity has subsided, the woman, the child, the man with the broom gone.

I can't go out there. I'd have to lie, to bow and say, These are my parents who raised me so well.

It's begun to rain. Fat drops bounce off the fire escape. The rain is drumming. It's falling heavy and lush. The telephone rings. Emily will come by with a cheesecake.

"I didn't make them. They were on sale at Ziggy's and so I bought two. I guess I shouldn't go shopping when I'm hungry. But I thought you might like one."

"I'd love one."

"I could drop it off. I still have the car out."

"I'll make you a cup of tea."

"Oh, I don't need any. Don't put yourself to the trouble."

"Yeah. It's hard work chopping firewood, Mom."

The rain has darkened the trees along the alley. Their leaves shine. *Esther, visit me.* Muriel presses her nose against the glass. *Esther, call me. Don't just tell me about the clothes you've bought. I need to speak with you. The other day when I dropped in it wasn't just to see Mom and Dad. You didn't come downstairs, but your radio was playing. Is Chris the only person who matters any more? I need to talk to you. Please.*

As well as cheesecake, Emily has brought a slice of parmesan, a bag of olives and two shirts. The striped shirt has become snug; the fuchsia one, Emily's decided, is more Muriel's colour. Muriel pours tea.

"I've decided I'm not going to finish my M.A. I'm dropping out. Do you want milk?"

Emily shakes her head at the pitcher of milk, covering her cup with her hand as a second precaution. "Oh, you have? You aren't going to finish?" Muriel always offers me milk, she thinks. To Muriel anything outside her own experience is unimaginable—enjoying clear tea, for instance. But perhaps that's how we all are?

"There's no point doing it, except to please Dad. I'm not interested in politics or economics."

"Does David know?"

"I'll tell him when I see him."

"He'll be disappointed but not angry. I don't think he'll be angry."

"I'm going to Africa." Muriel cuts herself a thick slice of cheesecake.

"You are? You never said. I don't remember you ever saying anything about Africa. Maybe, when you were little and you wanted to be a missionary."

"I only just decided. Right now. I'll get a job teaching. I guess that means I'll be gone two years."

"Two years? Oh, Muriel." Emily puts down her cup of tea. She smiles gently as her eyes explore Muriel's face. That Muriel's features are still recognizable seems to her a gift. "I'll miss you."

"It's not done yet."

The rain continues to fall. It is bouncing in fat drops off the metal stairs and darkening the trunks of the trees.

As Esther waits beside the bus stop the wind has succeeded in pulling her hair in every direction. She feels the sharp glances of strangers lifting her clothes. First they examine her legs, then they scrutinize her bottom, finally her chest. *I'll walk,* she decides. As she walks, she reads. The English moors spread out around her. A woman on a horse rides up to a cottage. *What sort of house,* she wonders, *will Chris and I buy? He'll want everything kept simple, and put away in its place. I'll learn to be tidy.*

At the red light the other pedestrians, mercifully, stare straight ahead, as though she were invisible. *Our house will be a bungalow. Chris will plant a beautiful garden. The most beautiful of any on the street.*

At the next intersection three of the corners are occupied by banks. Inside the bank with the bright green sign, on the northwest corner, her savings are growing, their tiny interest compounding. She imagines a bush bursting with delicate, diminutive yellow flowers. A forsythia. But however sweet the interest smells, it's mainly decoration and unreliable. Three-quarters of her earnings she deposits. She's crossed the street now. A small bell rings as she opens the door of the Milk Mart.

If there's anything left over when we've bought the house, perhaps we should risk buying some mutual funds. She chooses a blueberry-flavoured yogurt to take to work with her the following day. It is the one extravagance she allows herself. For David's birthday cake she buys Baker's chocolate and cream cheese. While the shop owner fits her purchases into a plastic bag, a large grey cat jumps from the window sill to rub against her legs. Esther pushes the animal firmly aside.

"I'm afraid I've never liked cats."

The owner leans over the counter. "Whiss, whiss," he orders. The cat disappears into the dark room at the back of the shop.

"Do you have any almond extract?" she asks.

For David's birthday she's bought him a silk tie and a book of crossword puzzles. These gifts, wrapped in gold paper, lie hidden in her dresser drawer. On a white card, she's penned the dark silhouette of a pine tree.

As soon as Esther steps out of the shop, the wind tugs her hair. It is only a short walk home now. The distance David used to walk to meet her when she'd stayed at a friend's or at the library until after dark.

How frail he's become. A slight hill leaves him breathless, though he won't admit it. I'll bake the cake after dinner, then call Chris. In the morning I'll ride the bus to work, inspected by the other passengers, and I'll try to ignore them. I'll wear my short black skirt and the brown velvet hat that belonged to Gram. If they want to stare, let them.

Only one block of houses remains and then she'll be home.

Squirrels run along the upper branches. The grass is strewn with acorns. The sun has warmed the park bench. Muriel rests her hands on the wooden slats. Couples walk arm in arm under the trees.

Damn you. Muriel stares at the lovers. She kicks at the acorns. One of the couples has stopped to kiss in front of the statue of King Edward on his horse. A long, tender kiss. Muriel closes her eyes, whether to shut them out or to see them better, she's not sure. What appears inside her closed lids is Esther, stepping from behind an oak tree. She's wearing a sundress and carrying a single daisy in her hand.

"Esther," Muriel shouts.

Esther plucks a petal from the daisy. "He loves me." She plucks another. And another.

"Esther," shouts Muriel.

"Don't give up," Esther calls, and she vanishes behind a tree. Muriel picks up an acorn and throws it at the statue of King Edward. The acorn lands in the grass, two meters away from her own feet.

At the edge of the park stands a red mailbox. Muriel tugs a large brown envelope out of her bag, and holds its weight in her hands. She reads over the address to be sure she's not left anything out. With any luck they'll accept her, and in six month's time she'll be living in Africa—in a country named Tanzania. She knows nothing about the place. She'll have to get a few books from the library. What grades will she teach, and what will her bedroom look like?

Don't ask, just go. Go quickly.

She walks along the edge of the park. A green metal garbage container has been provided for the public. Muriel takes from her purse the two halves of a blue envelope addressed to her father. She tosses them into the metal container.

The house where Esther lives stands on a corner, its garden wrapped around it. The Pacific Ocean is a fifteen-minute walk away, through quiet side-streets. Chris has moved the shrubs closer to the driveway. He's planted geraniums in two window boxes, set out pots on the verandah. Frost is rare there. I imagine the air as smelling of salt. Daffodils grow at the feet of the oak trees.

If I knew more about Esther, I'd tell you more. I'd tell you everything.